MOON'S BLUES

C.H. SPRAGUE

SILVER BEECH PRESS

Moon's Blues
Second Edition
2 3 4 5 6 7 8 9 10

ISBN-13: 978-0692539866
ISBN-10: 0692539867

"There are moments, Jeeves, when one asks oneself, 'Do trousers matter?'"

"The mood will pass, sir."

The Code of the Woosters, P.G. Wodehouse

CHAPTER ONE

Non datur ad musas currere lata via
There is no royal road to Art.

It stands to reason that you don't need to have the blues to play them. I mean, I'm sure B.B.King had his share of suffering, but really, once you've salted away the odd million or two, the blues must necessarily be at least mitigated, wouldn't you think?

These were the sort of thoughts drifting through my mind as I practiced holding down the strings of a G chord on my new guitar. If you're surprised to learn that I was even giving thought to the blues, perhaps a bit of explanation is in order. For those of you who imagined that the House of Duggie would enter into a glorious era of serenity and satisfaction following the events of last summer's softball tournament, which turned out well for me even though we lost, because at the end Jenny told me she was going to keep me under closer supervision, and, as far as Jenny's concerned, I'm all for the closer the better, let me just say that for a while I, too, thought things were finally looking up for Douglas C. Moon.

But as it turns out, Fate was just having one of her little jokes. At the time, of course, I didn't see the punch line coming. For those first three weeks, when Jenny was with me almost every day, I was as high as I believe it's possible to be without smoking anything. Then, on the last night in July, we were sitting outside the shack drinking beers and shooting the breeze. Jenny was tickling Orson under his chin, and he was purring like a snooze alarm. I should mention that Orson is a grossly overweight Persian cat, who was foisted upon me by Phoebe shortly after the tournament. She claimed it would be good for my soul to adopt an abandoned cat, and I was feeling so on top of the world that I allowed this travesty to come to pass. Rufie is still in a state of shock. The creature has shown a complete disregard of pet decorum, brazenly snacking out of Rufie's bowl while he watches. I'm surprised he hasn't throttled the feline already, but then, Rufie, like me, follows the knight's code. We don't throttle the pint-sized, no matter how much they may deserve it.

At any rate, there we were. Jenny was gently scolding Orson for having eaten another cricket. He can't get enough of them, and it being late summer in Virginia, they are on the march, chirping incessantly. I can almost sympathize with Orson's penchant for pouncing on them. They seem to be asking for it.

So, where were we? Ah yes, I remember feeling almost guilty because, well, you know, the world is full of suffering and injustice and whatnot, and there I was, not rich in conventional terms, but, although I'm no longer an under-paid Latin teacher, I still find solace in the old saying: *homo doctus in se semper divitias habet*—a learned man always has wealth within himself. At that moment, I was smiling at the stars, feeling like the luckiest man in Rapidan County. When Jenny put her hand on my thigh and squeezed, I leaned over to kiss her, but she pulled back and said, "Duggie, there's something I have to tell you."

If I'd been listening closer, I suppose I could have heard Fate snickering. As it was, I just smiled at Jenny, anticipating that she was about to reveal some embarrassing moment from her youth, some awkward confession of girlish fantasy.

"Duggie, you know I've been out of work since Shitley fired me at the tournament."

I nodded. It hadn't been one of those quiet, no-hard-feelings, pink-slip firings. It was a public, shouting, insult-exchange type firing. There was applause from those who witnessed it.

I waited for her to get to the point, like a sitting duck, unaware of the hunter slipping closer through the marsh grass.

"Well, I can't go on like this—being unemployed."

I stared at her, wishing I could tell her we could live on my salary, but let's face it, I can barely live on it myself.

"So, I was talking to Miles at the café yesterday—"

"Who?"

"Miles Brandon. He's the artist who's renting Hickory House this summer."

"Oh. Must be nice."

"It is. I went up there this morning to talk to him about a job. He needs an assistant to handle his e-mail, answer the phone, do errands." She paused and gave me a look. "He's going to pay me really well."

"You've already taken the job?"

"You know there aren't any good jobs out here. And this will only be for a few months until he goes back to his villa in France."

"He's got a villa in France?"

"That's where he spends the winters. He showed me some pictures of his studio there. It looks amazing."

"Oh." I sensed this wasn't the supportive reaction a good boyfriend should provide, but really? I felt as if I'd just swallowed a handful of crickets, and they weren't agreeing with me. "So... this Miles guy... he must be successful."

"And how. Some of his sculptures have been bought by museums. But he's not stuck up. He's funny and nice."

3

The way her eyes shone when she said this set off the warning buzzer in my head, but I still clung to the good old hope. "So, he's an old guy?"

"No. He's our age."

"Oh. Great," I managed to say, but I'm pretty sure she could tell I didn't mean it. I had actually seen this Brandon around, buying toothpaste at the Gas-n-Go, and though I didn't let on to Jenny, it was clear to me from the way the salesgirls swooned over him that they had been profoundly affected by his PBS accent, his chiseled profile, and disheveled mop of thick black hair. I suspect he dishevels it on purpose, if you want to know the truth. Be that as it may, the guy has a kind of style, I suppose. All right if you like that kind of thing. Ask anyone. They'll tell you I'm not conceited about my looks. I know they're in the average range—not a gargoyle, not a god. But even so, if it came to a mano-a-mano with Brandon, I think I could almost take him if it weren't for the eyes. His are the kind of sparkly, sky blue that made Mel Gibson rich. Plus, he's got eyelashes like a girl. Seriously. I wouldn't be surprised to learn that he uses mascara. So. All in all, not the kind of guy you want your girlfriend hobnobbing with on a daily basis.

But of course I couldn't say anything. *Vir sapit qui pauca loquitur*, as the fellow said. Know when to hold your tongue.

After she left, however, I felt as if the night grew darker, the stars seemed farther away, and even the crickets seemed to have shut up. It was spooky. No doubt all in my mind. Still, if it hadn't been so late I would have trotted up the path to Morris's house to see if he could offer some sage counsel. But I thought it would be sager on my part to wait till morning, so instead I smoked a joint and tried to think of other things. I'm pretty sure I did too, although of course I can't remember what they were now.

Morning brought no relief. When I arrived at Morris's at a decent hour, midway between nine and noon, there was no sign of him. Car gone, etc. Then I remembered that he'd mentioned something about a book tour last time we spoke, and I wished I'd been paying closer attention. Did he say he'd be gone a week, or six weeks? I trudged back down the path, trying to cheer myself up by whistling under my breath, but the only song that occurred to me was "Born Under a Bad Sign." Not much help there. Still, maybe it was the rhythmic tramping on the path, or the joint I smoked once I got back to the shack, but within an hour I had a brilliant idea for how to get rid of my blues. All I needed was a guitar. And someone to teach me how to play it.

I found Alvin kneeling in the sunshine on the back porch of the house he shares with the other guys in his band, on the sunrise side of Pignut Mountain. He was pouring milk into a saucer, and three cats were trying to get their heads into it at the same time.

"Hey," I said. "When did you become a cat man?"

He stood up and shrugged. "I don't know, man. They just keep showing up. I don't know where they come from."

"Do you want another one?" I asked, thinking Orson might enjoy being part of a gang.

"Hah. No thanks. I think three's my limit. It's like girlfriends. If you have too many, you can't keep any of them happy."

I let this go. As a musician, Alvin has never lacked for female companionship. It doesn't hurt that he's got the kind of winsome good looks that have made Brad Pitt's life such a walk in the park. Alvin's got the cheekbones of a supermodel and the unshakable self-confidence of a super hero. Women hurled themselves at him with a regularity that would have been annoying if he hadn't been so generous. When we were roommates in college, he would sometimes try to offload some of his excess on me, but generally speaking, the kind of girls who flock to the front of the stage tend to lack a certain, how shall I say, depth. Which never bothered Alvin, of course, since he was never a lad for serious discourse. But for me, well, it was all moot, since my heart belonged then, as it does now, to Jenny.

However, I hadn't come to Alvin for advice in matters of the heart, even though mine was certainly a bit off-kilter at the moment. Alvin may be shallow when it comes to women, but when it comes to laying down a solid rhythm and doing it all night long he's a pro. Musician, I mean. In college he was always in some band or other. I haven't exactly kept up with his most recent configurations. You know how these bands are. They're like those chemical substances that are inherently unstable. The slightest thing can send them spinning out into the cosmos in search of whatever it is they're looking for. I doubt any of them really knows. It takes more than matching tattoos to keep a band together.

Anyway, I figured if anyone could teach me to play guitar, it would be Alvin. He's boiled it down to its essence. He'd pretty much have to, since he's always completely ripped when he plays. So, that works for me too. My kind of guitar teacher.

After I explained my mission, he shook his head and said, "Duggie, I don't know. I'll help you get a guitar. And I'll show you some chords. I can get you started. But, man, it's not as easy as it looks."

I scoffed at this. "How hard could it be? You taught yourself, didn't you?"

"Well, yeah. That's my point, man. It ain't like Latin. You were always good at Latin, no question. But the blues... I don't know. You can't really teach 'em. You gotta feel 'em."

I put a hand to my chest and said, "That's why I know I can do this. Because I'm feeling it. Now. This is about Jenny. She's working for this artist, and I know he's gonna put the moves on her."

"What artist?"

"His name's Miles Brandon. Kind of a Hugh Grant clone."

"Who Grant?"

I frowned. I should have realized Alvin never watches movies. "Never mind. It doesn't matter. The point is, I want to learn to play so I can show Jenny that I've got soul, you know. I want to show her that I'm an artist too."

"Duggie. How long have we been friends?"

"Long enough," I said.

"That's right. Long enough that I can tell you, as a friend, man, you're not a musician. You can hardly carry a tune."

"That's what the guitar is for. I won't have to sing. I can just play."

He smiled at me in a condescending way, and if I could have thought of any other plan, I might have walked away right then. But I had to put aside my pride, for Jenny's sake.

He shrugged and grinned at me and said, "Okay. If you really want to do this, let's go get you a guitar. You got money?"

Damn. There's always something.

CHAPTER TWO

Faber est quisque fortunae suae
Every man is architect of his own fortune.

It's often puzzled me why people go to fortune tellers. I mean, obviously no one can predict the future. Or, if they could, they wouldn't spend their time at carnivals, holding hands with complete strangers for a few bucks a pop. But my point is, knowing the future...why bother? For instance, if you know everything's going to turn out peachy, well fine. Lucky you. But you still have to get through the intervening days, in all probability absorbing life's random blows in the process, and just because you believe you're going to land on your feet in the end doesn't make the fall any more enjoyable. And of course, on the other hand, if you get a bad prospectus, it doesn't make it any easier to take a punch just because you can see it coming.

All of this is by way of saying that when Jenny told me she had some news, I was just as glad I hadn't known it was coming. I mean, some people seem to get something out of pre-emptive suffering. Not me. I prefer to avoid any and all suffering until there's nowhere left to hide. But two days after I talked Glory into giving me an advance so I could buy a guitar, I was suffering like all get out. It's funny.

When I think of all the times I've watched guitar players at concerts or in bars, and they always make those faces like souls in torment while their fingers scamper nimbly up and down the strings, I assumed they were enjoying themselves. Now, as I'm trying to ignore the bleeding blisters on the tips of my fingers, I wonder if I misread their expressions of agony. Alvin warned me my fingers would hurt for the first few days. But this can't be right. I can hardly roll a joint.

I decided to take a break, and called Witty to see if he'd like to hang out. He's always ready to mooch off my stash, and he's been moping for the last month since Rosalie went back to France. These times between romances are hard on the Wittster. Although you'd never think it to look at him, with his pro-wrestler physique and hardened biker demeanor, Bob "Witty" Whitmore has a heart as mushy as one of those romance writers whose works line the grocery shelves. Each time he falls under the spell of some girl, he's convinced it will last forever, and when, after a month or two, love's flame sputters into ash, he wallows for a while in his misery. Lately, since Jenny has been spending more time with Brandon and less with me, I've turned to Witty for solace. He's not all that comforting, actually, but the sight of his gloom reminds me that at least my girlfriend is still within reach.

Witty suggested we go to hear some band at the Wrecking Ball. Having nothing better to do, and unable to face the prospect of touching the guitar, I agreed to go. The Wrecking Ball is one of those dives in Charlottesville where carefree students in the first flush of being able to drink far from their parents' watchful eyes tend to discover their limits. The music is loud, the lighting dim, and the women abundant in number and variety. Perfect for Witty, one would have thought. But as we sat crammed in a booth drinking our microbrews, he scowled past the multitude to the stage area where a determined foursome of skinny, eyeliner-wearing youths were doing their best to thrash the life out of the three chords they seemed to know.

"I thought you said the band was supposed to be good," I yelled across the table.

"This isn't them," Witt shouted back.

"This isn't who?"

"The Troll Models."

"Ah. Do you want to go someplace else?"

Witt heaved his shoulders with a look of disdain. "What's the point?" he bellowed.

"Maybe we can find a better band?"

"They're all the same," he grunted, slamming his empty tankard on the table.

I could see the alcohol wasn't doing anything to improve his mood. I patted my shirt pocket meaningfully and said, "Let's go to the park."

He kind of rolled his eyes, but he knows what "go to the park" means, so he stood up and followed me out. We didn't talk on the short walk to our favorite bench, the one that sits high above the greensward but is kind of hidden under a humongous oak tree, so you can see people coming, but they can't see you. Perfect for the swift inhalation of soothing herb.

In the flickering street light filtered through the leaves, Witty glanced at the joint and said, "Hey. Did you roll that thing in the mud?"

"Oh, you mean the spots? It's just blood."

"Yours, I hope."

"Yeah." I took a long hit and held it for a moment before I continued. "Playing the guitar is a lot harder than it looks."

Witty coughed for a few seconds. "Well, duh. If it was easy everybody'd do it."

"Doesn't everybody? It sort of seemed like it in college."

"Yeah, well, that was a long time ago, man. What are you trying to learn to play for now?"

"I've got to do something. That Brandon guy is using his arty charisma to undermine Jenny's feelings for me. I'm afraid if she keeps hanging around him, she's going to wish I had some talent."

Witty chuckled. "And you think learning to play "Stairway to Heaven" is going to impress her?"

"I was thinking more along the lines of "Lovesong.""

"Who did that?"

"The Cure."

"Never liked them."

"Jenny likes them."

"Yeah, well, I think it's nuts."

"What?"

"You. Playing guitar. It's too late for you, man. Look at your fingers. That's gross."

"But I want Jenny to see me as an artist."

Witty shook his head. "Man. Have another toke. You're not the artistic type, Duggie. Don't kid yourself. But you know what? Jenny doesn't care. She likes you, for whatever reason we'll never know, just the way you are. You don't know how lucky you are."

"Yes I do. But did you know that guy has a villa in France? And he's going to try to get Jenny to leave me and go there with him."

Witty exhaled laughing. "He's got a villa in France? Man. I'd leave you for him."

"Thanks for the support."

"Ah, quit your whining. She hasn't left yet has she? You just gotta be cool. Don't panic."

I nodded and looked out at the park below us. The evening was cool and pleasant, with just that hint of fall in the air. The leaves were rustling on the branches above us. Stars twinkled in the dark sky higher still. Every few minutes the door of the club far below us opened, and a surge of throbbing rhythm rose on the breeze, but neutered by the distance, like the tribal chanting of a cannibal group that had gone vegetarian. The edge of menace blunted.

I was feeling fairly blunted myself by this time, and when Witt suggested we call it a night and go home, I seconded the motion.

The drive back through the rolling foothills of the Blue Ridge never fails to work the kinks out of my soul. So much so, in fact, that by the time we neared the outskirts of Dudleigh and came upon the crowded parking lot at the firehouse, I felt my second wind kick in with a rush.

"What's going on in there?" I asked.

Witt leaned his head out the window and read the handmade sign tacked up on the wall outside. "Says there's a dance."

I pulled the truck into the parking lot and turned off the engine. "Sounds like there's a band."

We looked at each other, and without another word, we got out and went over to investigate.

Hairy Larry was manning the door. More beard than man, Larry is a fixture on the local music scene, always claiming to have found "the next Dave Matthews Band." Every man has to have a dream. We paid our five dollars and stepped into a sauna of sweat and patchouli. The crowd, of maybe two hundred, was doing the kind of dancing that doesn't require actual partnerage—just a kind of jump and spin and wave your arms around kind of thing. Great for someone like me, who never quite got the hang of the more complex routines.

The music was coming from the back wall. Witt and I worked our way through the gyrating masses to get a glimpse of them, and, contrary to the usual law of such things, the closer we got the better they sounded. The guitar player was sailing on some harmonic high of his own, while underneath him the bass player, drummer and a guy on keyboard were laying down a turbo-charged groove, which set knees shaking and heads bobbing all around us. There were the usual swirling psychedelic-style lights that HarLar always insists upon, but they seemed appropriate for a change, as opposed to when they're deployed in a bluegrass situation, as HarLar has been known to do. Maybe it was my current stoned state, but up closer to the band, I felt that rare euphoria, the kind we took for granted when we were kids just starting out. These guys were good. And they looked good. And when the singer, a pleasant looking swain with a bit of Sir Lancelot in his hairstyle, began to sing about the difficulties of finding a lasting meaningful relationship, not in those words, of course—I don't recall what it was he actually said, but I remember it sounded very sincere—I looked over to catch Witt's eye, and he gave me a nod that confirmed my estimation. When the song ended, the crowd cheered lustily, me among them. Then the lights shifted and the band began a slower tune, and from out of the shadows a girl stepped up to a second mic set a bit behind the lead singer and began to sing backup. She wasn't all that tall or anything, but when she began to sing "take me baby" in that kind of sexy voice, while she moved her hips the way no man can, well, all I can say is, I didn't think about Jenny for the entire length of the song. When it ended, the girl shook the shiny black hair that fell to her shoulders in loose curls, and gazed out at the crowd with ice blue eyes that glittered in the spotlights, and I had a flash of premonition.

I turned from the radiance on stage and saw it reflected in the mute worship on Witt's face. I tried to catch his attention with a wave, but I knew it was a wasted effort. He was full fathom deep, and past caring, infatuated with whatever her name was.

Delilah, as it turned out. The significance of this moniker wasn't lost on me, but I didn't bother to point it out to Witt. Something told me that in his current, freshly-dumped state he would neither appreciate, nor willingly believe, that this girl had trouble written all over her. Witt's not much of a reader.

When the band took a break, he bolted to the stage area. I followed at a slower pace. There was no way to head him off, but there was always the hope that she had a guy already. Though in my experience, it has seemed that girls such as her like to keep a stable of hopefuls on the side as a preventative measure to keep the main man in line. When I caught up to Witt, the girl was listening to his impassioned plea with an amused expression. At this range you could feel the pheromones shimmering in the air around her. Her face was flushed, a young goddess reveling in her own power. Standing around her were three young bucks in leather pants and tight shirts, their eyes glittering with undisguised lust. Witty seemed oblivious. As I got closer, I could hear him throwing his heart at her feet, and I could only hope she wouldn't laugh as she stepped on it.

When he finished speaking, there was a slight break in the action, like when the power blinks during a thunderstorm. I held my breath. With a throaty chuckle, she stepped forward and put a hand on Witty's chest and said, "You're cute. Don't go away." She topped this with a dazzling smile that set off a ripple of testosterone among the faithful. Then she turned and went off to join the guitar player, who was waiting with a bored expression by the stage.

Witty noticed me then, and grinned at me. "Did you see that?" he said.

I nodded. The other hopefuls watched Witt with baleful eyes. Clearly they didn't welcome new members in their ranks, but I guess the queen's word was law, as they didn't make any moves to drive Witt away. As if they could. They were all skinny, pasty and young, the kind of guys Witty used to make short work of in his wrestling prime, and I had no doubt that even now, out of training and with the beginnings of a paunch, he could dispatch all three of them even if they set upon him as a team.

"What a woman!" he said.

"Yeah. She's something," I said.

Witt frowned at me. "I know what you're thinking. And it's none of your business."

"I didn't say anything."

"You don't have to. I know you, Moon. You think I'm making a mistake. Blah, blah, blah. Just forget it. She's the one. I can feel it."

"What about Rosalie?"

"She's not coming back. And I'm not going to France. What would I do in France? She was never right for me. Just a summer fling. That's all over and I'm glad. Because now I know she left for a reason. Delilah. It's destiny."

If you could have seen the glaze in his watery blue eyes as he said this, you'd understand why I didn't bother to point out that this was almost the exact same thing he says every time he meets the next "love of his life." Besides, what did I care? I had nothing to do with this band. It wasn't like Rosalie and that whole wheels-within-wheels scenario with Glory's prize chef Eduardo and trying to keep him from finding out about Witt's romance. Thankfully, this time, I had no stake in this crazy scheme. If he wants to play with fire, I don't have to worry if he singes his eyebrows. Or anything else.

So, I said nothing, trusting that in the fullness of time he'd come to his senses. After all, *amoris vulnis idem sanat qui facit*. The wounds of love are cured by love itself.

After we parted and I was driving back up the mountain, I rolled down the window to breathe in the night air. It had that kind of damp leafy scent that always reminds me of being a kid in Falls Church, kicking through the piles of leaves on the streets when we'd go out trick-or-treating in the dark. Good times. But the memory kind of brought me down tonight. Not because my trick-or-treat days are long gone, but because I knew Jenny wouldn't be at the shack. Brandon had some art opening in D.C. that he wanted her to go to, and she'd told me she wouldn't have time to be with me. So this is how it was now. Autumn leaves. Jenny not here. I took a deep breath and wished I'd brought along a joint for the ride home. I needed to change my head around. I'm normally not a gloomy guy, but I gotta say, by the time I pulled the truck up to the shack, I was wishing

Morris was home. I could have used his counsel, patronizing as it may be.

I stepped out of the truck, and Rufie bounded up to me barking happily. I hugged him and instantly felt better. Then I noticed a shadowy figure sitting on my porch, and as my eyes adjusted to the dark I saw that it was Morris, just the man I wanted to see. I walked over and sat down beside him and asked, "How was your trip?"

"It had moments," he said.

I couldn't see his face very clearly in the dark, but I know Morris well enough that I could tell he didn't want to talk about his trip. Usually when he comes over this late, he wants one thing, and, as it happened, that was the very thing I wanted right then, so I went inside and rolled a fat one and didn't ask him any more questions until he'd had a few minutes to achieve lift-off.

When we were both pleasantly buzzed, I said, "A lot's happened while you were gone."

"Really?"

I waited for him to ask me for details, but he's a lot better at waiting than I am, so after about a minute, I started telling him about Jenny and Brandon, and my guitar. I considered mentioning Witty and the new girl, but I decided to hold off on that.

After a few silent minutes Morris said, "France, eh? It's beautiful there at this time of year."

I gritted my teeth. I knew that I had to expect him to toy with me before he offered any concrete advice. I rolled my shoulders and tried to relax the muscles in my neck. One of the problems with relying on Morris for sage counsel is that, as an author, he tends to analyze every situation in terms of plotting and characterization. Sometimes this is a good thing. But sometimes you just wish he'd cut the crap and say something helpful. Still, I know how lucky I am to have him for a friend, so I try to pretend I'm not needy.

"I'm really not interested in France," I said.

"You should be."

"Why should I care about France? The point is, how can I stop Jenny from going there if this guy asks her to?"

"It would be a great opportunity for her."

"Whose side are you on?"

"I'm simply pointing out that if you really care about Jenny, you would want her to have the best life possible, wouldn't you?"

I seethed silently. I could see what he was doing, of course, and naturally, you can't argue with his logic. But is logic everything? After a moment I said, "Of course I want her to have the best of everything. But I want her to have it with me."

"Hmm. You're going to need some cash to get a villa in France."

I sighed. "If you don't want to help me just say so."

He didn't respond for several minutes, and I was starting to think he was up to his usual mind games, when he said, "How are the guitar lessons coming?"

"I'm not taking lessons."

"Ah."

"Alvin showed me some chords."

"I see. And that was sufficient?"

I sighed. "Not exactly."

"Do you have a plan?"

"I thought I did. But I don't know. It's not as easy as it looks."

"Planning?"

"The guitar. Maybe if I'd started when I was younger. But now I don't have time to get good at it. I need to have something to show Jenny soon."

"Maybe you should get yourself a band."

"How am I going to do that if I can't play?"

"Bands need managers."

I sat back and considered this. It opened an entirely new line of thought. I had never managed a band. But I've been team captain for years, so I've got experience managing players. Whether it's music or softball, surely the basic principles apply—one for all and all for one sort of thing.

"But how do I get a band?"

Morris stood up and stretched. "I can't help you there. Why don't you ask your guitar teacher?"

He started down the steps.

"You're leaving?" I said.

"It's been a long day for me, Duggie. I'll be around. If you find a band, let me know. I'll come give a listen."

I thanked him for the idea, and he disappeared up the path through the woods to his house. To be honest, I was glad he'd gone. He'd given me much to think about, and I didn't want to press my luck with him. That's the thing about having a guru next door. You have to feed off the crumbs of wisdom he scatters in your path. If you push Morris, he can clam up for weeks.

I had a few more tokes to assist thought, and within minutes I had a good one. I'd ask Hairy Larry if he knew of any up-and-coming bands who were looking for a visionary manager to guide them on the path to success. I considered that HarLar might be disinclined to give away any trade secrets. But weighing against that would be his *cacoethes loquendi*, his inability to keep his mouth shut.

CHAPTER THREE

Saepe ignavavit fortem ex spe expectatio
Expectation based on hope often deludes courageous men.

The next morning being Sunday, I was on brunch duty at the café. When Glory loaned me the money for the guitar, she included this bit of business in the fine print, and at the time I didn't think I would care if I had to get up early on Sunday mornings. With Jenny busy at her new job I expected to be at home with a good book most Saturday nights. But last night had been an exception to this chaste regimen, and I was feeling a bit drained when I showed up to set tables and wash dishes.

"You know, I don't expect much from you at this hour of the day, but would it be asking too much for you to comb your hair? I don't want to frighten the customers." The look of disdain on Glory's face as she delivered this critique was nothing new. Years of brusque comments from this big sister had hardened my otherwise sensitive exterior, so to ignore this chaff was effortless. She didn't let up, however. Her tendency to dominate has flourished since she bought the café after her divorce. I sometimes think it's a kind of extended therapy. Since losing the wastrel husband she could never control, she has turned her iron will to transforming this once run-down little roadside café into a gastronomic landmark, and with the acquisition of her masterful Cuban chef Eduardo, her quest for a fourth star in the DC regional restaurant guide is near completion. Glory expects the food critic to sneak in incognito any day now, and as a result, she gets a little testy when she thinks the staff isn't holding the banner high enough. To give you an idea of how serious she is about this, she's totally forbidden me to smoke anywhere near the café, even during the long break between lunch and dinner, which seems a bit extreme to me. However, a little discretion goes a long way. If I limit myself to a couple of tokes behind the boathouse, she doesn't seem to notice.

She bustled away and came back with a large comb and held it out to me. "I'm serious. Go look in a mirror," she said.

I took the proffered comb and trudged off without a word. If I didn't owe her money on top of everything else, I might have argued just out of sibling habit, but as it was, I figured there was nothing to be gained by antagonizing her. Looking in the mirror, I could see her point. My hair, which is longish, dark brown, but not long enough for a ponytail, looked a bit more shipwrecked than usual. I wet the comb and pulled my hair away from my face in the manner of Antonio Banderas, and when I returned to the dining room, Glory gave me a tight-lipped nod. I never take these things personally. She's always on edge just before the place fills up. And as soon as the rush is over, as long as there haven't been any incidents, she usually lightens up and jokes around with the staff.

When the last big tipper had waddled out the french doors to the parking lot, she strolled over to the sideboard, where I was clearing the buffet table, and said, "So, how's the guitar coming?"

I hesitated. Having come to the decision to become a band manager rather than a rock star, I saw no reason to keep torturing my fingers with practice. But I had a feeling Glory might be a tad irked about the three hundred dollars she had coughed up for the guitar.

"Well, it's harder than I thought it would be," I said.

"Isn't everything?"

"So true. *Per aspera ad astra.*"

She glared at me. She never likes it when I pull out a morsel from my certamen days. She thinks I'm trying to show off. Nothing could be further from the truth. I'm the soul of modesty. Ask anyone. But there's no denying that the Romans had a way with words. It's not my fault I happen to know them.

"If you say so," she muttered.

"Actually," I said, figuring there was no point in delay, "I've decided the guitar isn't for me."

She frowned. "Is that right? Does this mean you'll be returning it to the store and getting my money back?"

"I don't think that's an option."

"I'm sure it is. That's how things work in the real world. If you spent more time in it, you'd know this."

Sarcasm, the stock in trade of all vibrant sibling exchanges. I couldn't respond in kind, however, due to my subservient position in the economic order. Working for your older sister has some benefits, but it ties your hands to some extent. I tried the old soothing smile.

"What are you grinning about? I'm serious. What's preventing you from selling the thing?"

"All in good time. I'm working on a new plan."

She heaved a sigh. "Fine. Just don't tell me about it. I have work to do." And with that, she turned and headed off to the kitchen.

I was glad she hadn't wanted to hear all about my new plan because, quite frankly, I needed some time to get the thing started. I had a few hours before the dinner shift kicked off. I hung up my white jacket and went to find Larry.

The road through Dudleigh is a two-lane affair with a few winding offshoots, some of which lead up to the mountains, while others meander toward the river. Most of the businesses in town sit along the main road, but a few individuals attempt to lure paying customers off the highway, and HarLar is one of these. In a weather-beaten, wood frame house a stone's throw from the Tin Toad, he operates a sort of knick-knack clearinghouse called Antiqua. The beauty of the antique racket, for someone like Larry, is that no one really polices these things. After all, who's to say what's really an antique, and what's a piece of garbage? It's one of those eye-of-the-beholder type things. *De gustibus non est disputandum.* One man's trash is another man's cherished curio. Of course, some people sell genuine old things that are worth a lot. But you won't find stuff like that at Antiqua. Larry tends to have cardboard boxes full of old 78's, chipped china, and dusty framed photographs of dead strangers. It always amazes me the stuff people will buy.

Larry likes the business, because he can scrounge stuff at yard sales and then mark it up and wait for suckers. It's a kind of low energy, low investment type enterprise. Most of the time he just lurks in the shadows of his musty old store like a furry spider in its web, spinning deals with the local bands he books into clubs as far away as Charlottesville.

I walked over from the café and pulled open the screen door, which screeched like a barn owl. Compared to the warm sunny day outside, it was dark and dank in the store. As my eyes adjusted to the lack of light, I saw a massive shadow shift at the back of the room, and as the swivel chair creaked and his rotund form rotated through the sliver of light that sliced through the dusty air, I saw that it was HarLar himself, wheezing softly like Jabba the Hutt.

"Lar," I said.

"Duglet," he said. "What brings you to Antiqua?"

He pronounced the word as if it were the name of some distant planet, accenting the first syllable.

I shot him the old pleasant smile, because it never hurts, and told him I was thinking about getting in the band management business and wanted to know if he had any advice. You see, I wasn't going to come right out and ask him if he knew a band I could manage. There's an art to getting someone to help you, and the first step is the butter. Applied liberally. Everyone likes to be asked for advice. Even if they claim it's annoying. At some deep level, everyone thinks they have advice worth taking. If you ask someone for advice, chances are they will think more of you because you've demonstrated the good sense to recognize them as being wise in some way.

Once the prospect is sufficiently buttered, you can slip a request into the mix that might have met with an instant rebuff without the good old grease.

"The most important thing to remember about bands is that they never know what's good for them. Never. That's fact number one."

"Really?" I was honestly surprised. "Why is that?"

"Because they all think they know what they want. They want to get famous, sell a lot of records, make a lot of money, have a lot of sex, the whole enchilada. But they never understand that the road to success is paved with boredom and drudgery. A lot of drudgery. And boredom. Repetition. Repeatedly."

I nodded. "Yeah. Okay. So... how do you, as a manager, help them cope with that?"

He belched loudly and patted his stomach. He looked at the can of Jolt in his hand. "I started drinking this stuff to kick the coffee habit. Now I'm addicted to this." He tossed the can across the room. It missed the trash can and fell with a clatter on the floor, where it came to rest next to several others of its kind. He looked at me. "You can't help them. That's the thing. All you can do is book the gigs and tell them where to go and when to be there. And then it's up to them." He shook his head ponderously, like a man watching a slow motion ping-pong match.

I waited, hoping he would expand on this theme, but he seemed content to let it end there. After a few minutes during which the only sound in the room was that of a fly buzzing furiously against the dirty windowpane, I tried to get the ball rolling again.

"So. What if the band's really good, and they're working really hard, and things are going pretty well, but they still aren't making any money? How do you handle that?"

"If the band's good, and they really want to make money, they have two choices. Either they have to get themselves signed by a label, which doesn't happen much anymore. Or they have to make their own records and sell them themselves, which takes a lot of work, and luck, and maybe, if they're lucky, and they're good enough, maybe they'll make it."

I nodded some more. Then I sat there as if I was thinking about what he said, although, frankly, I knew all that stuff already. Who doesn't? But I was hoping that by now he might be receptive to my real question. So, I waited a few more minutes and then I said, kind of casually, like it had just occurred to me, "Say, do you know any bands who are looking for a manager?"

A flicker of interest glittered in his small dark eyes. "You think you can manage a band?"

"I don't know. Seems like it might be fun."

He snorted. "Some people think wrestlin' gators is fun."

"Is managing a band the equivalent?"

"Gator wrestlin' is for wimps."

"Aah."

He lowered his chin and peered at me from the bristling hedge of eyebrow that shaded his face. "Gotta be a hardass, Duglet. Those skinny drummers? Those whiny guitar players? They'll leave you for dead if you don't let 'em know who's boss."

I swallowed. The thought flitted across my mind that perhaps this was to be yet another half-baked plan best tossed in the shredder. But then he smiled and said, "So you want to manage a band, eh?"

"Well, I—"

"You might be able to. If you get the right one. They're not all bad."

"Well, I don't know. I don't think I could wrestle an alligator..."

"Ah, I's just kiddin'. Most of these guys are harmless. Give 'em some dope and they're easy as pie."

I brightened. This was more like it. A band like pie. That's what I had in mind. "Well, maybe—"

"Tell you what," he said, leaning back on his swivel chair so that his stomach seemed to swell like a cartoon blimp. "You know that band you heard last night? They could use a manager. They don't know it. But they're not getting anywhere on their own. I'd take 'em on myself, but my plate's full right now. I got six bands I'm workin' with, and I can't take on another unless I dump one of them, and I'm not ready to do that just yet. It's five guys and a chick. They got some original material. They live across the river. If you can persuade 'em to give you a try, you can see if you're cut out for it."

"Do you think they would? I mean, I don't have any experience."

"Nobody has experience at the beginning. I can help you get started. Give you a few contacts."

"You'd do that for me?"

"Sure. They're a good band. Got potential. They just need someone to ride herd on 'em. Who knows? Maybe you're the guy." His smile shone like a brush fire flaring up in his beard.

"Well, great. That sounds perfect."

"I'll give you their number. Just remember: don't call before noon. Ever."

"Really?"

"Just kidding. You're probably safe after eleven thirty."

As I strolled back to the café, I was feeling pretty smug. I hadn't expected such rapid success, but here I was with the phone number of a band that I had heard already, and liked.

I flipped open the cell phone that Glory had given me for my birthday. I never wanted one of these things, but now that I had it, I realized it was the perfect accessory for an up and coming manager.

The band should be wide awake by now, and I was eager to set the wheels of fate turning in this new direction.

I went over to the giant willow that grew behind the Tin Toad and sat down in the shade to make the call. It rang for so long I was about to hang up, when a guy answered and said, "Your wallet's still here, moron."

I cleared my throat and said, "Um, hello?"

There was a pause. "Crater? That you?"

"Um. No. This is Duggie Moon. Doug Moon. I got your number from HarLar."

"Who?"

"Larry. Larry Stevens? The promoter?"

"The hairy guy?"

"Yeah. He gave me your number, because I'm looking for a band to manage, and I heard you guys last night, and I think I could help you."

There was a crash on the other end, and some scrabbling sounds, as if he'd dropped the phone. Then he came back on and said, "Who are you?"

"Doug Moon. I live up the mountain."

"And you're a manager?"

I hesitated. Much as I wished I could reply in the affirmative, I felt that it would be a bad idea to begin our professional relationship on a half-truth, so I said, "I'm just starting out. Larry's kind of taken me under his wing, showing me the ropes and all."

"Huh. Well, I don't know. We're not looking for a manager."

"Tell you what. How about if I come over to your place and talk with you all about what you want, and we'll take it from there."

"Huh. I gotta to talk to the rest of the band first. Give me your number. We'll call you if we're interested."

A minute later, after giving him my number, I hung up feeling a bit discouraged because I suspected he didn't write it down. I remained in the shade for a while, waiting for the phone to ring, and, to rid my mind of negative thoughts, I had a few hits from the skinny joint I had brought along for the ride home after work. Just enough to take the edge off. It made all the difference. I glanced up at the clear blue sky, where a few puffy white clouds were drifting toward the horizon, and I felt that, come what may, I had taken my first steps toward a new career, and this was something to celebrate. A new beginning, as it were. And whether or not this particular band elected to choose me as their manager, I felt confident that I would be the answer to some band's prayers. Assuming that they prayed. However, I would prefer not to manage a Christian band, not that there's anything wrong with them, but I suspect they might not accept me as I am, and like anyone, I work best in an atmosphere of mutual trust and respect.

I was musing contentedly along these lines, when a sort of electronic growl began in my pocket. I looked into it and noticed that the phone was set on vibrate mode. I certainly didn't recall setting it that way. Then I decided I should probably answer it, and I had a moment's doubt because of being slightly more ripped than I would have liked to be to present myself as a sharp business agent, but I couldn't ignore the call. If it was Glory, she would lecture the hell out of me if I didn't pick up, so I flipped the thing open and said, "Hello?"

A voice like a silvery mountain stream said, "Hello. Is this Duggie Moon?"

"Yes."

"Hi," she said, in a lilting sort of way, adding more syllables than one usually hears in the word. "I'm Delilah Page, with Identity Crisis."

"Oh. I'm sorry."

She laughed, musically, like wind chimes in a breeze. "That's the name of our band."

"Oh, sorry. I heard you last night, but I never caught the name. Good one."

"We're going to change it. But that's not why I called. Jimmy told me you want to be our manager."

"Yes. That's right. I would."

"Well, we might be interested. Why don't you come on over to the house, and we can discuss it?"

"Great. When?"

"You could come now."

"Oh." I clutched at a willow branch dangling nearby, but it snapped off, and I began to swish it in the air as I talked. "Well, I have to work in a few hours. Would it take long, do you think?"

"Listen, if you're too busy to come over, maybe you're not the manager for us."

I swished the willow branch rapidly back and forth so it made a little cartoon zipping sound. "I can come now. Where do you live?"

She gave me directions to a spot about five miles away on the other side of the river, on one of those windy roads that snakes up through the woods. I glanced at the time on my phone and did some rapid calculations. I would have to get a move on if I was going to make it back to work on time. I told her I'd be there in half an hour, hung up, and jogged to the truck.

The drive across the river is normally one that I enjoy, but on this trip the scenery didn't grip quite the way it usually did. In my mind's eye, I kept running over the image of Delilah, and that alluring way she had of breathing into the microphone, and the way Witty had snapped at the lure. I wondered if this might lead to difficulties between us, if I became the band's manager. I could envision scenarios in which Witty's desires might run counter to their best interests, and there I'd be, caught in the middle again.

As the house came into view, I shook my head and reminded myself not to worry about things which might never happen.

A trio of dogs came pelting down the stairs of the porch when I parked the truck. I smiled, feeling that a band that keeps dogs would be predisposed to like me. And, by extension, Rufie. Although, as they came upon me, this dog unit struck me as a bit on the rough side. The leader looked to be a mix of Rottweiller and mastiff. Sort of dark and droopy, but with rather more teeth than one feels should be necessary for the mere mastication of food. Add that he was attempting to put his paws on my chest in what may or may not have been a gesture of welcome, and I have to say I was a bit taken aback.

"Diesel! Come back here!"

A pale skinny guy stood on the porch, staring with a bored expression at the canine welcoming committee. The dogs turned and trotted back to the porch. I started walking toward the house.

"You the manager?" The guy gave me a flat look, as if I were selling magazines door-to-door.

"Yes," I said with an ingratiating smile.

The guy turned away like a teenager avoiding a confrontation with an overly inquisitive parent. He opened the door and went in. I followed right behind him, as he yelled up the stairs, "Delilah. The guy's here."

He left the room, and I stood alone in what appeared to be the living room-slash-practice studio. I glanced around. There was a shabby, orange couch along one wall. Aside from that, the only other furniture was an assortment of black speakers in various sizes, several guitars, a keyboard, and a set of drums. A threadbare Turkish-style rug covered with a fine layer of dog hair lay on the floor. The room had the dense cigarette and spilled-beer fug of a cheap bar.

"That was quick." Her voice lit up the room like a flaming arrow, hot and dangerous.

I stared at her and swallowed. She was dressed in a low-cut purple top of some sort of clinging material that clung to her in all the right places. She wore tight black pants and black leather, knee-high boots that laced up the front. Her hair was hanging all around her face, and her spangly earrings tinkled every time she laughed, which was often, as if she found the sight of me amusing.

She held her hand out to me. "So," she said. "I'm Delilah Page and you're Duggie Moon." She narrowed her eyes and gave me a long look. "Are the rumors about you true?"

I hesitated. "What rumors would those be?"

"I heard you're a pothead."

I faltered. Of course it was true, but no one had ever confronted me with it so directly. Certainly no one of her rock-star goddess caliber.

I shrugged. "Well, you know how it is. You smoke one joint and you're addicted."

She laughed. "You're funny. I like that in a man."

I smiled, but I was worried that she wasn't going to see my serious side, so I said, "Thanks. But, seriously, I think I could be a good manager for your band."

She put one hand on her hip and cocked her head at me. "And what makes you think that?"

"Well... I've listened to a lot of music, and bands. My college roommate was in a band, so I know a lot about what that's like. The band lifestyle, I mean."

"Uh huh. And that's it?"

I could see she wasn't finding me so amusing now, and as I wracked my brains for some winning phrase I remembered the pitch. "Well," I began, "the thing is, I know that I have a lot to learn about the music business. But I've been a team captain for years, and in that capacity I've had to deal with difficult personalities and tense situations and, you know, the kind of balancing act you have to do to keep things going when you're dealing with demanding situations. Pressure. That's what I mean. I'm good at working under pressure."

The lines in her face smoothed out as I said this, and she looked at me with a kind of twinkle in her eyes and said, "How do you know it's not the pot talking?"

I blanched. Then I thought, what the hell, there was no point in pretending to be someone I'm not. "Well, that's always a possibility.

But even if that's true, the point is, I can be unflappable when it counts."

She giggled. "Unflappable?"

"Yeah, you know. Cool. Whatever."

She shook her head and studied me for a moment. Then she sort of bit back a smile and said, "Tell you what, Mr. Moon. You get us some gigs, and we'll see how it goes. We'll pay you something for your trouble. But we're not going to make this official until we've seen some proof that you know what you're doing."

I nodded. "That sounds fair. Just give me a chance. That's all I ask."

"Well, all righty. You know where we are. Give us a call when you've got something lined up."

"You won't be disappointed," I said as I started toward the door.

A funny shadow seemed to cross her face, and she said, "I don't get disappointed. I get revenge. It's never disappointing."

I looked to see if the twinkle was still on the job in her eyes, but there was no sign of it.

CHAPTER FOUR

Aut viam inveniam aut faciam
Where there's a will there's a way.

By the time I finished my shift at the café later that night, I had begun to feel the slight clutch of queasiness that precedes the full onset of panic. For the fact that I really had no idea what the first step was in managing a band had gradually forced its way past the guard dogs of optimism who usually prevent negativity from sticking its leaden foot out to trip me. The evening stars were sparkling away in the velvety night and all that, but I couldn't enjoy them. All I could think was, how do I show this band that I'm the can-do manager they need?

Just to show you how stumped I was, the answer still eluded me even after I had finished the other half of the reefer I'd saved for the ride. And, although normally I would have turned to Morris for advice, I felt that he'd given me a push already, and he probably expected me to do a little work on my own before I came back for another dose. As I stepped into the dark shack, I knocked up against the guitar, and it went crashing to the floor with a hollow twang. I turned on the light and was relieved to see I hadn't broken the thing. And then, as if the light switch had triggered something, I realized that Hairy Larry must be chock full of ideas, and surely, since he already knew this band, he would be able to get me started. I considered calling him right then, even though it was late, but decided instead to seek him out in his lair in the morning.

Came the dawn, or in my case, seven-ish, when Rufie gets restless and starts pulling the covers off me, I awoke full of the will to win. But I figured it would be too early for a man like HarLar, so I took Rufie for a walk. Now that Jenny's sister Amanda is working for a graphics place in Charlottesville, she's given up her part-time job as my dog walker and plant custodian, which is just as well, since I don't have the money to pay her, thanks to Morris arranging to have my pot bus hijacked, and thereby spoiling my summer fund-raising scheme. I'm not angry, of course. As it turned out, Morris's swift work kept Sheriff Quayle from nailing me for possession with intent to distribute. All's well that ends well, as they say. But they never take into account that after things end, well, they keep on going. Especially the need for money. Really, the fellow who said *pecuniate obediunt omnia* knew whereof he spoke, and the lesson still holds. Money wears the pants in this life.

I was musing along these lines as I pulled up to the diner, the cheap eats side of the café, which Glory still operates for the morning business. There's no place else in town where they make a decent cup of coffee. I saw Eric's truck in the parking lot. He met Amanda when she was working the counter at the diner. Now that she's got an apartment in Charlottesville, he still haunts the scene where his romance began. Although they're a happy couple, Eric worries constantly that Amanda will meet some smooth-talking architect or landscape designer and be swept off her feet. I tell him not to worry.

I sat down beside him. He nodded at me, and we drank our coffee in silence for a moment or two. I sensed that Eric was in one of his moods, and I was content to wait him out, confident that he'd burst into revealing personal anecdotery soon enough.

He heaved a loud sigh.

"I'm thinking of moving to Charlottesville," he said.

"What? You can't do that. You'd break up the hearts league."

He turned on me impatiently. "Duggie, has it ever occurred to you that it might be time for us to grow up?"

I absorbed this without comment. I knew it was the anxiety talking.

"Amanda is making new friends at her job, and she's going out to bars with them after work. And... it's only a matter of time." He stared gloomily into his coffee cup.

"Until?"

His shoulders slumped and he said, "Until she realizes she can do better than me. A beautiful talented girl like her. And what am I? A two-bit carpenter."

"Don't sell yourself short. You're a very handsome two-bit carpenter. For someone your age."

He gestured violently with his right hand, spilling a fair quantity of coffee on the counter. I dabbed at it with a napkin while he ranted on.

"And that's another thing. I'm older than she is. A lot older. She's going to meet some hot young guy, and she's going to realize she's made a mistake, and then it'll all be over."

"And you think you can prevent this by clinging to her like a needy loser?"

"Obviously I wouldn't do that."

"Oh." I paused, giving him time to think. "Well, let's say you move to Charlottesville. You'd still be a carpenter, right? Or are you planning to go back to teaching? I suppose you could always teach English at one of the private schools."

He sighed again. I finished my coffee and said, "She loves you, man."

"How would you know?"

I shook my head. If he was determined to be miserable, there was nothing I could say that would shake him out of it. I decided to change the subject.

"Do you know anyone looking to buy a guitar?"

"What?"

"A guitar. My guitar. I need to sell it, so I can pay Glory back."

"I thought you just got it."

"I did. But you know what they say, buy in haste, regret at leisure."

He frowned at me.

"I'm not really regretting. I now see the guitar was just a step in the process of discovering my new career."

He raised his eyebrows in a weary way.

"I'm managing a band."

He made a sound which fell somewhere between a snort and a laugh.

"Since when do you know anything about managing a band?"

"Since yesterday, when I talked to HarLar about the idea."

"And he encouraged you?"

"Eventually. He put me in touch with a band, and I'm in the process of finding them a gig."

"Really? Are they any good?"

I could see his skepticism diminishing. I told him about hearing the band at the fire hall, and his expression changed to one of mild goodwill, more like the Eric we all know and love.

"That sounds good, Duggie. Let me know when you get something lined up, and I'll come."

"Yes, well. I'll let you know. Oh, and by the way, the next time you're talking to Amanda could you ask her if she knows any places in Charlottesville where they might want to hire a band?"

The goodwill vanished from his face. "Yeah. Sure. I really want to give her another reason to go hang out in clubs without me."

"You could do it together. To help me. She's always been nice to me."

He stood up and started toward the door. After a minute he looked back at me and said, "I suppose it wouldn't hurt to ask her."

"That's the spirit."

He shook his head. "See ya," he said as he walked away, but I heard him mutter "managing a band" in a kind of sarcastic undertone before he went out the door. I didn't care. He'd never even heard them. Or seen Delilah. I sat at the counter for a minute reflecting on the fact that Witty had seen Delilah, and that he might even now be concocting some insane plan to win her heart. Judging from what I'd seen of Delilah, when it came to hearts, she appeared more of a collector than a giver.

I lingered at the diner for another couple of hours doing the crossword from Sunday's Post until it was late enough that I figured Larry would be awake and open for business. But when I strolled over to Antiqua, it was locked up tight and a tiny sign, which I hadn't noted before, explained that the shop was always closed on Mondays. Temporarily stymied, I considered going back to the shack and relaxing with a bit of smoke, but my supply has been tight since the events of last summer. Now that the Sheriff has me on his radar, I've had to keep the home scene relatively clean. You never know when old Quayle might decide to stop by for a spot check. He'd have to have a warrant, I suppose, but Morris assures me there's no shortage of probable cause and that I need to be on my guard. A total bummer.

As a result, I've been seeing more of Darren, relying on him for my supply. But it was too early in the day to try to find him either, even if I had any idea where he actually slept. Legend has it that he keeps a sleeping bag behind the Killer Zombie machine at the Bust-a-Gut, but that place doesn't open until three, so I couldn't verify the rumor.

Then I remembered that Alvin might well be awake, and what with being a musician and all, he surely wouldn't be at work, and what was more, he might have some helpful advice to offer on the topic of finding gigs for the band. Plus, there was a better than even chance that he'd have some pot. I got in my truck and headed over the mountain.

After a few pleasant hours with Alvin and his bong, I had a plan. He suggested throwing our own gig. All you have to do is hire a hall and print up some flyers, and get somebody to man the door. Easy peasy. He knew of a few places I could look into renting, so my next step was to make some calls.

This turned out to be a lot harder than you'd think, since none of these places appeared to have what you might call a live human on the premises. By the time I finished leaving messages with a half dozen answering machines, I felt completely spent. It was almost four o'clock by then, and I decided I'd done enough for one day, especially considering that it was my only day off from the café.

Rufie and I went out for our usual walk. The late afternoon sun was flickering through the hickories, and the trees were just starting to turn a browny yellow like butterscotch. Rufie crashed along in the fallen leaves, scaring up birds and squirrels. The air had that kind of peaty aroma, and the breeze carried the scent of burning leaves. Autumn in Virginia. Close enough to perfect for a guy like me.

Yet, when we got back to the shack and I had finished off the remains of the mac and cheese, I sat out on the old porch with a beer and a reefer and watched the light fade from the sky, and for some reason, I couldn't shake this strange feeling, entirely new to me, that there was something missing. Of course, not having Jenny there was the big thing. But, in a way, that space where she was supposed to be had been empty for so many years that having it empty again almost felt normal. Having her around for those few weeks was amazing, but the whole time I don't think I ever really believed it could last. It was like being on vacation in some tropic paradise—or how I imagine that would be anyway—you know it's too good to be true. Now she was gone again, and things were the way they'd always been. Only it was kind of worse, because now I had the memories of what it was like to have her here. The comparison, you see?

Rufie came over and put his paw on my knee and looked up at me. He can tell when I'm thinking about Jenny. "Yeah. I'll be okay," I said, patting him. "I'm just a little blue."

And, I kid you not, I got shivers up my neck as I said it. I put down the beer and went in and picked up the guitar and brought it out onto the porch. I hadn't touched it in a couple of days, so my fingertips had healed a bit. Still, I winced preemptively as I attempted to hold down a G chord. The pain was bearable. I gave the strings a tentative strum. The result was a bit jangly, and perhaps not strictly in tune, but it soothed me like a kick in the head. In a good way, I mean. I rearranged my fingers and tried a C chord. Again, a slightly twangy but somehow satisfying racket. I plunged ahead with the linchpin, the D chord. And then I played them in sequence, in something approaching rhythm, while banging my foot on the porch, and after a few minutes of this I felt something let go in my chest, the way you do when a nice buzz first lifts off. So what if I had the blues? At that moment I was happy, because at last I could sort of play them. Who knew?

CHAPTER FIVE

Fere libenter homines id quod volunt credunt
Men readily believe what they want to believe.
Julius Caesar

Came the dawn the sunny optimism for which I am well known had returned to full force. As I pulled into the café parking lot, I was singing along with Aretha, who was recommending the pleasure to be found riding on the freeway of love, and I couldn't agree with her more. I stepped out of the truck, finishing the last chorus solo, and nearly bumped into Eric, who was leaning against his car with his hands over his ears. I gave him a look. He's known me long enough to be aware that his lack of musical taste renders his critiques null and void.

"Are you through?" he asked, taking one hand away from his ear.

"I've only just begun," I replied.

"Fine. I'll make this quick then." He pulled a folded paper out of his jacket pocket and thrust it at me. "I only came here to give you this," he said.

I scanned the thing quickly. It was one of those brightly colored flyers you see tacked up on telephone poles, announcing a Battle of the Bands in Charlottesville. I gave Eric another look, this one quizzical.

"It's for your band," he explained. "Amanda said the club owners in Charlottesville go to these things and look for talent."

"Hmm," I said, reading the thing more carefully. "It's in two weeks?"

"Yup."

"I don't see anything on here about how much they pay. It just says there's a prize for the winner."

"They don't pay you to play. You have to pay to enter the contest."

"How much?"

"I think it's a hundred dollars."

"Ouch. The band's not going to like that idea."

"You should pay it, to show you believe in them."

"Huh. Easy for you to say. I have no ready funds at the moment."

"Can't Glory loan you the money?"

"I already owe her three hundred for my guitar."

"Can you sell it? You aren't actually playing it, are you?"

I frowned. Whether or not I was playing it, the truth was, last night I formed a bond with my instrument. I wasn't ready to give it up. "Maybe I can get Glory to spring for another hundred," I said. "The restaurant's been pretty busy lately. She must be doing okay."

"Great." He turned to get in his car. "Let me know if your band's gonna play. I'll bring Amanda. We'll cheer for you."

That raised another question in my mind. "How do they pick the winners anyway?"

"The audience decides. Whoever gets the loudest cheers, you know?"

I watched him drive off and stuffed the flyer in my back pocket. It wasn't the sort of gig I'd been hoping to offer the band, but it was a start. I went to ask Glory for another loan.

I realized as soon as I got inside that it would have to wait until after the luncheon fray. She was in full-tilt hostess mode, oozing charm and geniality to all and sundry, but I knew the c. and g. wouldn't extend to the hired help, even if related by blood ties. The place was packed to the beams with some sort of group, the Rotary Club or its like, and Glory was working the room, chit-chatting and chuckling like the proverbial jolly innkeeper.

Later, when the place had cleared out and I was cleaning off the tables, I caught her eye and asked if I could have a word, and the geniality vanished like a hot-buttered roll on Sunday. "What do you want?" she asked.

I cleared my throat by way of getting started, but before I got a word out she said, "Have you got my money?"

I gaped at her for half a second, wondering how to proceed, inasmuch as she had cut me off at the pass. I did another spot of throat clearing and said, "Well it's funny you should ask—"

"No, it's not. I'm dead serious."

"Actually, I haven't got the money yet. In fact, I was hoping you could loan me another hundred."

She shook her head at me in a kind of weary way and folded her arms. "I knew this would happen. This is the thanks I get for loaning you money in the first place. It isn't enough that I give you a job, and that I allow you to traipse in here whenever it suits you. What do you need more money for?"

"It's for a Battle of the Bands contest in Charlottesville. I want to enter my band to help them get hired by a club."

"You have a band now? You just got the guitar last week."

"I'm managing a band."

"You?" She snorted. "Duggie, normally I don't mind supporting your crazy schemes, but this isn't a good time. I've sunk every penny I have into this place, and we're still not making a profit."

"I thought, with Eduardo cooking—"

"Yeah, well. I thought so too. It's coming along. But not near fast enough. I'll be lucky if I can hold on until the holidays. If I can make it to New Year's, we just might survive."

"Oh. I didn't know. I wouldn't have asked—"

"Forget it. Now you know. Sorry. You'll have to find some other sucker to throw money at you. And if you do, see if you can get them to kick in that three hundred you owe me." She turned and marched back to the kitchen, leaving me to my thoughts.

These weren't as sunny as I'd have liked, so I decided to step outside and fire up the skinny spliff I had brought along for the mid-afternoon lull, in hopes that it might open a new line of inquiry re: funds. Stepping across the drive on my way to the secluded spot behind the café where I could find the solitude so essential to clear thought, I caught a glimpse of raven locks out of the corner of my eye, and felt that spark that only happens when Jenny's near. And, lo, there she was. This would have been just what the doctor ordered were it not for the fact that clamped on to Jenny's elbow was Miles Brandon. Although we hadn't been formerly introduced, his Prince Charming sheen was unmistakable.

Jenny beamed. "Duggie! I was hoping we'd see you. We just had lunch. Were you working?"

"Yes. In the back." I eyed Brandon uneasily. His grip on Jenny's arm showed no sign of weakening, and he was looking at me with a kind of dismissive impatience, as if he'd already seen enough of me.

"Oh, you haven't met," said Jenny. "Miles, this is Duggie." There was a sort of something in the little smile she flashed at him as she introduced me, as if I were a backward cousin who must be humored. I met Brandon's glance. It hit me like a sliver of ice slipped down my neck. But he flashed a perfect smile. I nodded in reply. I couldn't summon a smile.

Jenny didn't seem to notice. She was chatting on about some event Miles was taking her to in D.C. that night. I didn't catch the details. Before I knew it they were stepping into his black BMW, and away they went. I stood frozen in place for a moment or two. Then I continued back to the good old secluded spot. And by the time I'd finished most of the joint, I had reached that calm philosophic plateau where I do all my best work.

After all, as unpleasant as it was to see Jenny in the company of such a smooth Lothario, the fact that she introduced me to him by first name only suggested that she had already sketched out the fundamentals of our relationship. Naturally, he would view me as a rival, and one can't expect warmth and bonhomie from a rival, however cultured he may be. Thus, I had nothing to worry about. Except for this matter of the hundred dollars. And it takes more than a trifle such as that to stop Douglas Moon when he's on the march.

I leaned back against the willow and closed my eyes, the better to envision success.

Next thing I knew someone was shoving me. I opened my eyes and noticed that the sky was that inky shade of purplish blue that generally follows the sunset, and Witty was kneeling beside me.

"Are you trying to get yourself fired, man? Your sister's steamed."

I stood up quickly and started for the café.

"Hey, slow down. I need to talk to you," he said.

I paused. "Is she looking for me?"

"Not exactly. She was too busy to do it, so I said I'd find you."

"Ah."

"But you might want to work on your excuse before you go in there."

I sighed. There was no point in rushing in there if Glory was already mad. I might as well give her time to take it out on someone else first. "What did you want to see me about?"

"Eric told me you're managing that band. I want to go with you the next time you meet with them, so I can see Delilah."

"Have you talked to her since that night?"

43

"No. I don't know where she lives. I don't have her number. I need to play it cool, but I have to see her."

I sighed again. When he gets this way, the only thing to do is stand back and wait until the wreckage settles. "Fine," I said. "I was thinking of going over there tonight after work, but now I've got to go make things right with Glory, and that might take a while. She was already peeved with me before this."

"Why don't you just skip it? Let's go to Delilah's now. You can suck up to Glory tomorrow. She can't fire you."

I considered this. Even though I knew it was the testosterone talking, Witt's suggestion had appeal. I've always believed in avoiding conflict whenever possible, and in this case the choice was clear.

"Come on," I said, untying my apron. "I'll drive."

On the way to the band's house, I filled Witty in on the Battle of the Bands idea, and he leapt at the chance to get involved by putting up the hundred dollars for the entry fee. I was so grateful I lit up what was left of the joint and shared it with him, and by the time we got in range of the band's dogs, we were both feeling fairly merry and bright.

The buzz lasted right up until we got to the door and heard the crash of a cymbal. Peering through the screen door, I saw a beefy-looking guy sitting behind a drum set-up. He was glaring at a skinny guy with shoulder-length, dirty blonde hair. I knocked lightly and they both turned and scowled at the door.

There was a rustle, and someone stood up on the far side of the room, and I heard a silvery voice say, "Well look who's here. It's Mr. Moon. Come in."

I pulled the door open and stepped in. Witty came right behind me.

Delilah stayed where she was, studying Witty as if he were a menu and she wasn't sure if she was hungry. "Have we met?" she said to him.

"Yeah," he said, smiling like an idiot. "At the firehouse. You guys were awesome."

Some may find fault with Witty for his somewhat unpolished manner and blunt approach, but in this case his oafish words cast a soothing spell on the room. The band members clearly hadn't heard enough praise to have grown weary of it yet. They murmured thanks, while Delilah lowered her chin and held Witty in her gaze like a puma who has made her selection from a herd of bison. I'll say this for Witty, he may not be the world's most graceful or debonair male, but to a certain type of female a sturdy chin and massive biceps offer a kind of comfort mere intellectual stimulation can't match.

Delilah turned to me and said, "So, Mr. Moon, have you got us a gig?"

I launched into my Battle of the Bands spiel, talking faster as I felt the temperature dropping in the room. When I paused and said, "So what do you think?" it was purely rhetorical. From the groans and expressions of disgust, which the band freely offered while I elaborated on the details of the gig, I could tell they weren't taken with the notion of competing for public favor.

Of more concern was the fact that Delilah wasn't smiling either. There was a moment of awkward silence. I looked at the band. They looked at Delilah. After a minute she looked over at Witty and said, "What do you think, Big Boy? Should we do it?"

Witty turned pink and nodded, apparently robbed of the ability to speak by the sheer wattage of her pheromone spell.

Delilah raised her eyebrows a fraction and then shrugged lightly. "All right. We'll do it. But only because we haven't got anything better lined up. This isn't the kind of gig we're looking for, Moon. You'll have to do better than this."

I nodded eagerly. "I know. I know. This is just a start. I've got some better things in the works."

"Such as?"

I kicked myself. Inside, of course, where she couldn't see it. "Well, I don't want to say anything about them just yet. Don't want to jinx anything, you know. But I've got some things in the works."

She gave me a look blended of doubt and mockery, with a hint of threat. I maintained the good old confident smile and said I would be in touch soon with all the details for the BOB and more. Then I said we had to be going, ignoring Witty's mute plea, and we edged out of the room. I didn't breathe easily until we were a mile away. By then Witty had forgiven me for rushing him out, and was celebrating the successful encounter with his lady love.

"She likes me! I could feel it! There was definitely something there. Did you hear her call me 'Big Boy'?" He was nodding and bouncing in his seat like a little kid soaring on the sugar rush of cotton candy. Ah well, I thought. Let him enjoy his moment. God knows it can't last.

CHAPTER SIX

Frustra laborat qui omnibus placere studet
He labors in vain who tries to please everyone.

As I walked into The Barracks on the night of the event, a spot of vertigo kicked in, causing the room to tilt a bit until I got adjusted to the déjà vu and the din. Back in the day, when I was a restless undergrad at UVA, I frequented this dungeon regularly, as the doorman was known for his lax attitude in the matter of IDs. Now, gazing about me at what I assumed must be a largely college-age crowd, although they looked a lot younger to me, I was almost overcome with gratitude that I no longer had to rough it in the mating jungle. The haunted, hungry gaze of these youngsters took me back to a time when I was constantly looking for someone to take my mind off Jenny. Needless to say, I never found anyone.

I was glad to see that the place was packed. There would be no shortage of cheering fans. I looked around for the band but didn't see them anywhere. Presumably there was a backstage area, and I wondered if I should work my way there to give Delilah and the boys a bit of encouragement. But before I had a chance to push my way through the mob, a slender, rat-faced boy with hair gelled into a faux-hawk stepped onto the stage and began the proceedings. After an initial spate of rabble rousing, along the usual lines of asking repeatedly "Are you ready to party?" while the crowd responded with the obligatory roar of the well-trained mob, the MC rattled off the names of the six bands who would be vying for glory and five hundred dollars. I didn't catch the names of the other bands, aside from the first one, which was called Duplex.

Two young guys dressed in black t-shirts and mirror shades took the stage, each of them standing before a keyboard. The house sound system cut off, and the chanting of the small core of fans pressed up against the lip of the stage became evident. Spotlights turned on the duo, and a torrent of sound erupted from their equipment. To my untrained ears it sounded like a pair of dump trucks backing up in sequence, smashing into the odd garbage can along the way, and running over the occasional stray cat. There were no vocals to speak of, but there was definitely some sort of rhythm to it, as if a couple of mastodons were thumping through the primeval forest.

It seemed to last for an eternity, although, according to the clock over the bar, only twenty minutes had passed. When it ended, the musicians raised their fists in a power salute to their faithful, and melted into the darkness. I looked for someplace to sit down.

I was working my way to an empty barstool when I spotted Eric and Amanda standing at the back of the room. Amanda's eyes were glistening in the neon light. As I got closer I saw that the tears on her cheeks were from laughter.

"What was that?" she shouted, as I came in range.

"You mean the Duplex?"

"Is that who they were? What kind of music was that?" she asked.

I shrugged. "Techno Metal? I don't know. Takes all kinds, I guess." We managers have to be diplomatic in public. You never know who your next client might be.

Eric shook his head and looked back at the stage. "When does your band play?"

"I don't know. I'm kind of hoping they'll play near the end."

"Why?" asked Amanda.

"I have a theory that it's like the Academy Awards. The movies that come out late in the year always win, because people forget what came earlier. It's that short attention span thing."

"I don't know, Duggie. I think I'll be having nightmares about those last guys for weeks." Amanda shuddered and then laughed.

I turned back to the stage, where a nondescript foursome wearing rumpled, flannel shirts and torn bluejeans were plugging in their guitars. I didn't catch their name, but as soon as the first screaming guitar lick shot across the room, it was clear that they subscribed to the roadhouse blues-band ethic. They played driving 12-bar blues for twenty minutes straight, during which time the scrawny lead vocalist alternated between growling complaints about faithless women and piercing harmonica solos, in which a similar message was implied.

They were well received by the crowd, but they didn't worry me. Although they were competent, confident and not entirely repellant, their sum star power was dimmed by the conventions of their chosen genre. They did what they did well, but so do a thousand other bar bands. Next.

That was my view anyway. And I saw nothing to worry about in the next contender either, a six-piece country rock band with a pedal steel player whose volume effectively rendered the lead singer mute. We could see his lips moving. The expression on his face suggested good times and bad, perhaps lost dogs, trucks, wives, etc., but the details of these emotions remained a mystery. The crowd applauded anyway. By this time most of them had had more than one drink.

The last band before Delilah's was an ambitious bunch with eight people crowding onto the small stage, all of them wearing suits except the singer, a full-figured girl with long, wavy blonde hair. She wore a strapless gown, and I would have been worried if the size of her voice had matched the rest of her, but luckily, this was not the case, her vocal stylings being more in line with those of Minnie Mouse. The band was capable and I gave them points for song selection—one from column R&B, one from the swing era, one Motown, and a finale medley that ran from the Beatles to KC and the Sunshine Band. But they had sadly misjudged their audience. The Barracks regulars were never attuned to the slick and stylish. They liked their music raw.

So I was feeling fairly upbeat as the clock struck ten and Identity Crisis sauntered on stage. By then the crowd was getting restless. They were buzzing and milling like hornets wishing someone would jab a stick at them so they could have a reason to live. And out came Delilah.

She strolled to the middle of the stage like a Bentley purring past a line of stopped traffic. A hush came over the room. She looked out over the crowd. She didn't say anything. But you could see a small smile at the corner of her full, red lips. Then she raised the tambourine over her head and brought it down on her hip with a crash that jolted every male in the crowd, and Tucker started singing his standard opener, "Get Your Hands Off My Heart." Delilah didn't sing on this one, she just kept the tambourine shaking, and you could see it was having an effect on the crowd. They cheered enthusiastically at the end, and the band launched into "Take It If You Want It," the one I'd heard at the firehouse, where Delilah proved that the two little words "oh, baby" can out-lust a lap dance.

At the end of that number, the crowd went nuts. Then Delilah sang her solo number, "Was I Good?" Suffice it to say, the call and response feature of this one was ecstatically affirmative. And during the last two songs there was much joy in the room. I could almost feel the crisp hundreds in my hand. I caught Eric's eye and he gave me a thumbs up. It was as close to a sure thing as I've ever been in my life.

Which just goes to show. *Nihil est incertius volgo.* Nothing is more uncertain than the favor of the crowd. Of course, Cicero never managed a rock band. Still. He obviously understood the unpredictable nature of a mob.

What happened was, the sixth and final contestants turned out to be an all-girl, tribute band called The Dangles. Yeah. I think you can picture it. The lustrous hair, the skimpy outfits, the knee-high boots. Now add the salacious moves. I can't remember a single song they did after the first one, which was, if memory serves, "Be My Baby." Not that it matters. The mostly male crowd were salivating freely throughout the set, and when it was over, the cheers of the multitude did not go to Identity Crisis.

I went backstage to offer my sympathies to the band, hoping they might not hold me responsible for the bait and switch tactics of the promoter, who must have known all along that in a venue such as The Barracks a group like The Dangles would trounce anything but an all topless group.

I found the band out back in the parking lot. A glance was sufficient to tell me they weren't ready to laugh about it yet.

"I told you we shouldn't do it," said Crater Law, the drummer, a wiry well-muscled individual, who had the aura of a firecracker with a short fuse.

"We had it won until those chicks started flashing the crowd," said Tucker. He turned to me and said, "How come you let them go last? Everybody knows the band that goes last wins."

I nodded. "There was nothing I could do. The promoter dictates the line-up."

"Yeah? Well, you should have fixed it so we were last. We out-played everybody else, man." This remark, delivered in the quiet, slightly menacing tone of Jack Nicholson just before his fangs lengthen, came from Matt Poole, the bass player. It was the first time I'd heard him speak, and you could tell by the ripple of silence that followed it that the others agreed with him.

"Listen," I said hastily, "I'm sorry tonight didn't go the way it should have. You guys should have won. Anyone could see that. But it was still a good gig. You made some new fans—"

"But no money," Crater interrupted.

"Right. That's true. But I covered the entry fee, so you didn't really lose anything. And the next gig will be better. I promise."

"Yeah?" Delilah spoke quietly but there was no doubt she had everyone's undivided attention. "Tell us about the next gig, Duggie."

The challenge in her tone made my throat tighten up but I pressed on. "Yes, I'll be giving you that information real soon. Just have a few minor details to nail down and then I'll give you the whole scoop."

Somebody guffawed at this. I couldn't tell who. I was about to embellish on the theme of this gig, the details of which I could imagine now and revise later, when Matt stepped away from the circle and said, "Let's get out of here. He's got nothin'."

I opened my mouth to contest this, but they were already walking away. I decided it might be best to let Time the Great Healer do its work on the band's injured pride. In the meantime, I had to come up with something concrete to restore their faith in me. Not that they'd had any to begin with, but the fact remained, I still needed to earn their faith. But how?

I was leaning against a car, gazing up at the streetlights, lost in thought, when Witty came trotting over and said, "Where are they? You didn't let them go already, did you?"

"I didn't see any reason to stop them."

"I wanted to tell them how great they were. I wanted her to know I was here, cheering for her."

"Yeah. Well."

He frowned at the empty street. "Was she bummed about not winning?"

"What do you think?"

"They shoulda won."

"That was the general consensus."

"It's your fault. You should have made sure they went last. Everybody knows that."

"Yes. That was pointed out to me."

Witty leaned on the car next to me and frowned. "So when's the next gig?"

"I wish I knew. Unfortunately, I don't have anything lined up yet."

"Well shit, man. Why don't you go in there and see if the bar wants to hire them? They rocked tonight."

I gave this some thought. On the one hand, perhaps a good idea. But, on the other, somehow I didn't think Delilah and the boys would be eager to return to the scene of the crime, so to speak. Still, I supposed it was the sort of thing a manager would do. So I trudged back into the bar and eventually found the promoter who told me that they had already hired The Dangles to play for the next couple of weekends. I left by the front door, hoping to avoid Witty and any further advice. I'd had enough for one night and felt the need for some quiet time. I was confident that with the right stimulation I would hit upon a solution.

The trouble was I was running kind of low on the soothing herb. Then it occurred to me that, it being Saturday night, Darren would be manning the games at the bowling alley. I got in the truck and was just backing out when there came a pounding on the door, and I nearly swallowed my tongue, until I recognized Witty's big head glaring at me through the window. I rolled it down and said, "What?"

"What's the big idea? I was waiting for you to come back and give me the update."

I chafed a bit. But then I told myself it was only natural. Ever since he kicked in that entry fee for the band, Witt seems to feel that he's part of the management team. I could have set him straight, I suppose, but I know from our years together in college that it's more trouble than it's worth to try rational persuasion. I explained my current mission, and he frowned and said, "You know, you're gonna have to straighten up to do this job right."

"But not tonight," I countered.

Any hope I had of getting Darren to make a deposit in my reefer reserve faded shortly after I tracked him down at the bowling alley. He assured me he had what I wanted, but he wouldn't get off work until one a.m., and I would have to wait till then. Normally I would have hung around. But it had been a long day, and the stress of fending off the band's ire had left me depleted. I headed home emptyhanded.

When I stepped out of the truck, I expected Rufie to come bounding over to greet me, as is his custom. But for some reason he didn't, although I could hear his tail thumping against the porch floor with a happy sort of rhythm. Then I noticed another silhouette lurking beside him, and a hint of Juicy Fruit in the air, the signature scent of my stalker.

"Hey," she said. "Where've you been? I tried to find you after the battle of the bands but you disappeared. So I came here to wait for you, but you took so long I was just about ready to give up."

I sighed inwardly. I have nothing against Phoebe. And her girlish enthusiasm for my company has, at times, lightened my dark moments, but at this particular dark moment, I would have preferred to see the glowing light of a fat joint, and I was fairly certain she didn't have one of those on her person.

"Your band should have won," she said.

"Yeah," I said. "They thought so too."

"I guess they weren't very happy."

"Not so much." I sat down on the chair next to her, trying to think of a tactful way to ask her to leave. Because, honestly, although I appreciated her obviously good intentions, I wasn't in the mood for a chat. I sighed a bit loudly in the hope that she would take the hint. She reached over and patted my leg. I flinched. This Phoebe, I should remind those of you who stepped out for a smoke during my recent brush with the law, has worshipped me from afar since the glory days of my certamen victories. All through high school, while other guys piled up trophies for football or track or what have you, I secured my footnote in academia in the field of Latin scholarship, which, for some reason, came to me *stans pede in uno*, easy as standing on one foot, as Horace used to say.

The realm of competitive Latin geekery is an even more arcane and smaller world than that of the Dungeons and Dragons crowd or the Final Fantasy set. Those of us who shone brightest in the Latin arena have little to show for it in the real world, except for the occasional rare groupie. Back in the day, Phoebe, who is two years younger than I, was awestruck by my Latin prowess. Though unbeknownst to me at the time, she has since made herself knownst, and I feel a certain responsibility to live up to her idealistic perception of me. She thinks I can do no wrong. And even though recent events have provided ample evidence that her theory is flawed at best, she continues to believe in me. Touching really. That's why I can't simply tell her to beat it when she shows up unannounced and uninvited.

However, just as I was about to tell her that I was going to call it a night she said, "I've got something that might cheer you up."

I cringed a bit at this. In my previous experience with her, Phoebe's ideas of cheering almost always involved pom-poms. But she reached into her pocket and pulled out a slender stick, and my heart leapt up when I beheld the reefer in her hand.

"I thought you didn't..." I faltered.

"I don't. But some guy at the shelter gave me this. He was so happy we'd found his dog. I was going to say no thanks, but then I thought of you, and I thought maybe you'd like it. If you don't want it—"

"No. No. It's perfect. Just what I wanted, actually. Things have been a little... um, tight lately, and... no, really, this is perfect. Do you mind if I light it now? Would you like some?"

"Ah, no thanks. You know I'm not into it. I hope it's good."

"One way to find out," I said, striking a match. A couple of minutes later I could attest that it was good. Very good.

"Duggie?"

I looked over in the dark. She was still there. "Yes?"

"When's the band playing again?"

I leaned back in my chair and gave this some thought. I wondered if it was too soon to go and ask Morris for a refill of advice. Of course, the walk through the woods to his house would be pleasant on this balmy night. There was just a hint of fall in the air, that slight smell of dry leaves and damp earth that suggests the back-to-school season. Glad I wasn't going back to school. No more teachers. No more books. Actually, I still like the books. But not right now. Right now what would be really great would be something to eat. I tried to remember if there was anything edible in the kitchen. Nothing came to mind. Then I remembered my guitar. It was in the house. I started to get up to go get it—

"Duggie?"

I turned. Phoebe was still there. "Yes?"

"The band? Do you know when they'll be playing again?"

I took a deep breath and gave this some serious thought for a few seconds. "Nope." I shook my head. "But if you hear of something let me know. They're a good band."

I turned and went in to get my guitar. I passed through the kitchen and ate a few crackers, and found a beer. When I came back to the porch, Rufie thumped his tail, happy to see me. I was happy to see him too. Phoebe wasn't around anymore, but that was okay. I don't think she's a blues fan. And sometimes a man's gotta play the blues. Me. I'm the man. A bluesman is what I am. Not everyone knows this. Except Rufie.

CHAPTER SEVEN

Aequam memento rebus in arduis servare mentem
Remember when life's path is steep to keep your mind even.
Horace

I didn't get a chance to consider the band's future until the next morning, after the first load of brunch dishes was in the washer. I had slipped out the back door and was sitting on the steps, trying to gather my thoughts, when a bony knee dug into my shoulder blade.

"I should have known I'd find you lurking here. There're still tables to be cleared, you know."

I cast the old ingratiating smile up at Glory, more out of force of habit than from any hope that it would soften her mood. When the café is busy, she tends to model her behavior along the lines of Napoleon. No time for tact. I rose to comply, but as I ambled past her, she grabbed my arm and said, "Hey. Did I hear right that you've got some sort of band now?"

"That is correct."

"Are you in it?" she asked, with a soupçon of skepticism, it seemed to me. I shrugged it off. These older sisters never tire of lording it over the hapless younger sibling.

"I'm their manager."

"Hmm." The skepticism ratcheted up a notch. I rose above it.

"Why do you ask?"

She frowned and gave me a long look, as if considering whether to slap me. Then Fate must have stepped in and pinched her arm, because the next thing I knew she was bending my ear about how she was trying to earn some extra dough by doing a little catering on the side. And I was standing there thinking, fine, good, but what does this have to do with me, when she got to the point.

"So, this client in Darlington is throwing a birthday party for her daughter, and she's hired me to do the catering, but now she just called and said the band cancelled on them at the last minute, and she wants to know if I can get her a band."

She looked at me with that 'don't-bullshit-me' expression so familiar from years of playing "I Doubt It," and I felt a wave of gratitude toward Fate and all the powers that be. I beamed at her. "You want to hire my band?"

"I don't know. Do I? Would they embarrass me? Would they steal the silverware? What kind of band are they? What do they play?"

"They're a six-piece rock band. They've got two singers, a guy and a girl who can sing anything. They just played in Charlottesville last night. They're really good."

She pursed her lips and looked at me. "How much?"

I stared at her for a minute before I got her drift. "You mean money?"

"Right. They don't play for free do they? I suppose that would be too much to hope for."

"No. Not for free. But they're very reasonable," I said, although a light sweat broke out on my neck as I ventured into the speculative portion of the proceedings.

"How much?"

I did some quick coin tossing in my head and said, "How about six hundred?"

She weighed this for a minute. "For four hours?"

"Four. Or five. They're versatile."

She mused another minute. "I don't suppose you have a tape or a CD I could listen to."

"Ah, no. We're working on that," I said, venturing deeper into the gray area between truth and possibility.

She sighed heavily.

"Just out curiosity, when is this shindig?"

"Next Saturday," she said, giving me a dark look. "If I do this, you have to come through for me. This isn't some fire-hall hoedown, where everyone is in cut-offs and Grateful Dead t-shirts. It's in a tent. The guests will be in tuxedos. There will be champagne. Horsey people. I can't afford to mess this up. Do you understand? If I trust you on this, you've got to promise me you won't piss in the well."

I nodded. I knew how much it would mean to Glory to make a hit with the swanky Darlington crowd. They were old Virginia aristocracy. If Glory gained their good graces, the café would be on the map.

"We'll make you proud," I said. I was sure of it.

When I finished up at the café, I headed right over to Delilah's house to tell the band about the gig. I hadn't let on to Glory, of course, but I had been reflecting on the band's customary attire, and I felt it might take all my reserves of diplomacy to convince them that for this particular gig it would be best to wear the jeans without the holes.

I found the band sitting in their kitchen talking. They fell silent at the sight of me, and from the looks on their faces, I guessed that my name had come up in the discussion, and not in a good way. But it takes more than a few bad vibes to daunt Douglas Moon. I flashed the brave smile and said, "How would you like to play for a private party in Darlington on Saturday?"

That got their attention. But, although they looked alert and interested, no one spoke until Delilah said, "Do we have a gig?"

"Yes. It's a birthday party in a tent." I went on to mention the tuxedoes and the whole "High Society" aspect of the job. I noticed Crater and Jimmy exchanging smirks as I suggested the idea of a dress code. When I paused for feedback, I looked at Delilah, but it was Matt Poole, the bass player, who spoke. "How much?" he said, in a voice like an ice machine coughing out a few cubes.

I cleared my throat briefly and said, "Six hundred. For four hours. Or five if you want."

Delilah sniffed. She glanced at Matt and said, "What do you think?"

Matt shrugged. "We don't have anything else to do."

A mumbled, muttering agreement followed this remark, and I let out a sigh of relief.

"Hey," Delilah said, looking at me. "So we'll do this. But this kind of thing isn't what we're about."

"I know that. This is just—" I hesitated, debating whether to let them in on my hopes to rent a hall and promote a concert for them. Then I decided they should know I wasn't just sitting around waiting for the phone to ring. "Actually, I'm working on setting up a concert for you guys at a bigger hall."

"Really?" A spark of interest lit Delilah's face. "That would be good. We'd like that, wouldn't we boys?"

The rest of the guys all nodded, and Tucker said "Yeah, we'll do this gig for you, Moon, to help you out, but we don't want to be just a party band. We want to build up a following and go out on tour."

"Right. Of course. Doesn't everyone?" I smiled. They didn't.

"All right, Mr. Moon. We'll see you in the big tent," said Delilah.

I shuffled out of the room and went out to my truck, escorted all the way by the dogs, wagging their tails and sniffing my pants. At least they seemed to have accepted me as one of the gang. Sooner or later the band was bound to come around.

By the time I arrived back at the shack, I was ready for some quality time with my guitar. I was beginning to develop calluses on my fingertips, and I was looking forward to playing sans pain. But as I got out of the truck, I saw a familiar figure waiting on the porch, and he was holding my guitar.

"Hi," I said. "Do you play?"

Morris gave me a look. "No. I don't. I leave the playing to the professionals."

"Ah. Well, I don't know if I'll ever turn professional but—"

"So it was you."

I paused at the foot of the steps. "Was me what?"

"I assume it was you making that noise late last night?"

I frowned slightly. Morris can get above himself at times. It comes from being a successful, published author and a college professor. His word carries a lot of weight on campus, and if he has a flaw, it is that he sometimes oversteps the bounds of common courtesy at home, that is, at my home, which is always open to him, of course, but that doesn't mean I have to take the kind of subtle abuse which he has been known to heap upon his hapless students.

Thus, it was with some reserve that I said, "If you are referring to my playing the blues, I hope you liked them."

A shade of what'sit passed across his face. You had to be quick to see it, but I've learned to read Morris like a book, and I could tell he was plotting.

He leaned back and cradled the guitar. "Actually I do like the blues. Lightning Hopkins. John Lee Hooker. Stevie Ray Vaughn." He paused. "Why are you trying to play the blues? I thought you were managing a band."

"I am managing a band," I said, taking a seat next to him, "but it's stressful. Playing the blues restores my soul."

He gave me another look. "So you're going to keep doing it?"

"Yes. I am. And I'm sorry if you don't like it, but this is my house and if I want to play my guitar of an evening, then that's what I'm going to do."

He nodded quietly. Then he said, "I see," and stood up, leaving the guitar in the chair, and began walking away. I could see he was set on being mulish about this, but I didn't want it to escalate into a full-fledged snit, so I said, "Hey you don't have to leave. I won't play while you're here."

He paused and turned his head toward me. "Comforting as that is, it won't solve the problem." He resumed walking toward the woods.

"So you're just going to stay away whenever I'm playing?"

"No. I'm going to have to soundproof my house."

Well, if you're worried about my losing Morris's company, don't. I know him. He has his little ways, as do I, and I've learned to accept it. Sooner or later he'll want to get stoned, and he'll come crawling back. Well, not crawling of course. Morris would never. But strolling for sure.

The thought of getting high brought me back to the as yet unsolved issue of my dope supply. Obviously, I couldn't expect Phoebe to come through on a regular basis. I was wishing I'd stuck around and waited for Darren, when I heard a tinny, muted version of the opening bars of "Born To Be Wild," the new ringtone on my cell phone.

"Hello?"

"Duggie? So, you really have a cell phone now?"

"Hi! How did you get this number? I mean, I'm glad you did. But, I don't think even I know it."

"Glory gave it to me. I went by the café tonight to talk to you. Glory told me you'd already gone. I tried earlier, but you didn't answer."

I had never heard Jenny's voice on a cell phone before, and, although it wasn't as good as having it right next to my ear, you know, being able to smell her hair and... Okay. Never mind. She was saying something.

"I'm sorry we didn't get by to hear your band last night. Miles had to go to an opening of a friend of his in D.C., and it went late."

"Oh that's all right. There'll be another gig."

"Soon?"

Something in the tone of her voice gave me that feeling you get in your gut when you're standing on a rocking boat.

"Um. Probably. Actually they're going to be playing at a private party in Darlington on Saturday. Maybe I could bring you."

"I don't know. Let me talk to Miles and see what's going on Saturday. I'd like to hear your band before I go."

"Go?"

There was a short pause. Then she said. "That's really why I'm calling. It's not going to happen immediately, but pretty soon, and I wanted you to know, because, you know, I don't want you to worry about me. Or us. We're fine."

"We are? Where are you going?"

"To France. With Miles. For a couple of months. Just for the winter. To help him with his work. And then I'll be back in the spring."

I held the phone, feeling as if a noose were tightening round my neck.

"Duggie? Are you still there?"

I swallowed and closed my eyes for a second, but that only brought up an image of Jenny with Miles Brandon. I could just see them, laughing together, drinking wine at his villa.

"Duggie? Are you all right?"

I opened my eyes and stared out at the dark woods. "Sure. I'm fine. I'll be fine." I gritted my teeth. A lot of words were fighting to make it to the exit, and though I tried to hold them back, a few got loose. "I'll miss you," I said.

"I know. I'll miss you too. But it's such an opportunity for me. I've never been to Europe, and Miles says we can take lots of side trips, because everything's so close over there. We're going to visit Paris and Barcelona and Florence." She sounded excited, even though I could tell she was trying not to.

What could I say? Don't go?

"That sounds great," I said.

"I'll see you before I go. We may not leave for a few weeks, or even a month. I'll talk to Miles about Saturday. I'll call you."

I hung up and stood there. Rufie came over and rubbed his head against my leg. I patted his head, but I couldn't speak. *Curae leves loquuntur ingentes stupent.*

CHAPTER EIGHT

Credula vitam spes foret et melius cras fore semper dicit
Credulous hope supports our life and always says that tomorrow
will be better.

Tibullus

Some people never feel at ease unless they have a sizable chunk of
cash salted away for a rainy day.

I've never been one to lose sleep over money. But after a long
night of tossing and turning without anything resembling rest, I rose
with the dawn, resolved to restore the natural order to my world.

This meant finding Darren, and he, of course, is never awake
before noon, so I had a lot of time to wait. I used it working on
"Sitting On Top Of The World," which may not be technically a
blues song, but it felt right, and that, I believe, is the whole point.
After a brisk walk with Rufie around the edge of the woods, I put in
a few hours on the old instrument, playing indoors so as not to
disturb Morris. Although I felt his critique of my endeavor was
unwarranted, I didn't want to piss him off more than necessary.

And this business of Jenny leaving the country... right. The
concept kept tripping me up every time I thought I'd gotten far
enough away from the moment when she told me about it to examine

it calmly. I mean, wasn't it bad enough she was spending all her time with that guy? Did she have to put an ocean between us?

Apparently so. Thus the urgency to score some pot. There was no substitute for Jenny. But that only made the need for therapeutic herb more critical.

When I finally tracked down the wild man in his place of employment, he at first caviled and said he couldn't take care of me right then, but I gave him the lowdown on Jenny, and he offered to fix me up if I drove. During the short roundtrip to his backwoods lair, I filled him in on my band and mentioned how I'd had no luck finding a place to stage a concert. And then Fate, in Her whimsical way, deigned to toss a crumb my way.

"Whyn't you use the Hangar?" Darren asked, as I parked the truck back at the bowling alley. We had smoked a sample joint on the return trip, and I was feeling significantly more optimistic about life in general.

"That place in the valley?" I asked. I had a dim recollection of a cavernous old building, formerly used by a small group of local airplane enthusiasts. I had once considered using it to try my hand at the, ahem, import business, until Eric talked me out of it.

"Yeah. They have concerts there. Nobody hassles you. You bring your own shit. It's great."

"Does it still have electricity?" I asked, though I was already thinking of generators.

"Yeah. The guy who owns it keeps it on. He's still got a few old planes out back. But there's plenty of room. And it's cheap."

"Isn't it kind of out of the way? Do people actually go there for a concerts?"

"Sure, man. You just gotta get some flyers printed up. Kids come from Charlottesville. It's a scene."

"Really?" I had no idea. I glanced over at Darren, noting the snake tattoo curling up his neck from under his shirt. I have never felt the urge to get tattooed, or pierced. I sometimes feel the dividing line between Darren's generation and mine is delineated by punctured skin.

But this idea of his had merit. "How much do you think it would cost to put on a concert there?"

He shrugged. "Depends. You got your own lights? Sound system? I don't know how much it costs to rent the place. It can't be much. There's no heat."

"Really? Doesn't it get cold?"

"Yeah. But pack a bunch of warm bodies in there and it's all good. Besides, once they've had a few drinks they don't mind the cold." He grinned.

He had a point. But it raised another concern. "Do they bring their own? I wouldn't have to get a liquor license would I?"

"Hell no. That's the whole point. Ain't nobody comin' around to check yer ID."

"I suppose not. Should I sell beer, do you think?"

"Get a couple kegs. A lot of cups. It's a sure-fire money-maker."

I nodded thoughtfully. The child spoke sooth. This could be the answer to my problems. A few flyers, a few kegs... nothing to it.

"Thanks, Darren. That's a good idea."

I decided to drive out to the Hangar. In my mind's eye, I seemed to recall a rusted hulk of a barn surrounded by a cracked sea of asphalt. The scent of motor oil and hay bales figured into it.

After a few scenic wrong turns, I arrived, and it was just as I remembered. A knee-high fringe of weeds zigzagged down the middle of the defunct landing strip. The place looked deserted but for a few cows grazing in the overgrown pasture behind the building. When I got out of the truck to take a look inside, I heard a banging noise echoing off the high, tin roof. I followed the sound and found a small man in grimy overalls, bent over the engine of a small tractor.

"Hello?" I said.

He turned his head and caught my eye and held out a wrench. "Hold this," he said.

I took the proffered wrench, and he said, "See if you can hold onto that clamp there while I knock the bolt off."

I did as he asked, having no clue when it comes to mechanics. He banged away for a few minutes, then swore quietly and straightened up and looked at me. "Wanna buy a dead tractor?" he said.

"Not really. Are the owner of this place?"

"You wanna buy it?"

"No. I'd like to rent it for one night."

"Lemme guess. Another one of them hippie parties?"

"No. A concert. With a band."

He looked at me. "Wouldn't be much of a concert without a band."

"Right. A friend told me that you rent this place out."

"That's right. When were you thinking of having this concert?"

"I haven't set a date yet. I wanted to be sure we could get the building first."

The man shrugged and wiped his hands on an oily rag. "The rent for one night is a thousand dollars."

"Whoa."

"You think that's a lot? Try gettin' a place this big anywhere else for less."

I cleared my throat and did some hasty math in my head. Say we charged ten dollars per person. We'd be in the clear after the first hundred.

"How many people can this place hold?"

"Five hundred easy. Six if they're friendly."

"And you've had crowds here that size before?"

"Yup. Got plenty of field parking."

"Ah. And as far as alcohol goes..."

"I don't care what you do, long as you clean up the mess afterwards."

"Great. So, do you need a signed contract or anything?"

"You give me a deposit. To hold your date."

"Okay. Great. I'll be back."

"I'll be here. If you don't see me, go on back to the house." He pointed to a small cabin at the far edge of the pasture, past the cows.

"Nice spot," I said.

He shrugged, and I had started to walk away when a thought occurred. I turned back to him and asked, "Is there a bathroom here?"

"Got one at the house. You'll want to get some porta-johns for your concert."

"Oh."

As I drove slowly homeward, I pondered the growing list of expenditures that would need to be managed somehow in order for this concert idea to succeed. I started ticking them off on my fingers—posters, rent of hall, lights, sound system, kegs, cups, porta-johns. Darren had made it sound easy, but I wondered whether, after all the costs were covered, there would be anything left for the band.

A lesser man might have given up at this point. But the Moons are not lesser men. We dream big. We are men, and women, of action. I've said it before and I'll say it again: *audaces fortuna iuvat*—fortune favors the bold. Delilah and the boys obviously didn't have a lot of faith in me yet. But after I get them an audience of six hundred screaming fans, they'll see me differently.

However, while my aura of invincibility remained on high, a shadow of concern nipped at my heels, for there was the daunting sum of a thousand dollars to be found somewhere. I couldn't ask Glory again, especially now that she'd revealed her own pecuniary straits to me. For a moment or two I considered asking the band if they'd be willing to forego their pay for the upcoming party gig so that I could use the money for some of the concert overhead, but I was fairly certain that this idea would be met with scorn, if not outright derision. No. It was clear that I had to come up with some brilliant plan. Yet, though the weather was inviting and my day was free, I was drawing a blank as far as possible investors were concerned. When I got home, I rolled a restorative reefer to assist the process of inspiration. And after I'd smoked it, I realized, of course, that I had nothing to worry about. Fate had brought me this far. Surely She wouldn't let me down when it came time to pay for posters and porta-johns. I simply had to have faith that the Wheels of Fate were grinding along, and the necessary grain would materialize when it was needed.

I took a deep breath and felt the inherent rightness of this view. There was nothing to be gained by fretful worry. I got my guitar and spent a happy hour playing the three chords I knew.

I had achieved a serene state by the time Witty roared up the drive. He got out and slammed the door of his truck, waking Rufie, who had been lulled into a pleasant doze by my guitar. Rufie fired off a few barks until he recognized Witt, then shifted to wagging his tail. Like me, Rufie is ever the welcoming host.

"Hey!" Witt said. "Did you go back to Delilah's house again?"

"Yes."

"Why didn't you tell me?"

"It didn't occur to me."

He snorted. "Come on, man. You know I'm trying to get with her. I can't just call her up."

"Why not?"

"Cause she's with that Tucker guy. The singer. He's not gonna let me get near her. That's why I need you to help me out."

I shook my head. "I can't help you. They're not going to welcome you because you're with me. They haven't made up their minds about me yet."

"Yeah, but you got your foot in the door, and that's all I'm asking. Just let me slide in with you until I can convince her to dump that pretty boy and be mine."

I rolled my eyes. "So you want me to let you know whenever I'm doing anything with the band?"

"That's right. You owe me."

I considered this. "That's true. But I'd owe you even more if you loaned me some more money."

"Huh? What do you need money for?"

I outlined the concert idea for him, and he was nodding like a bobblehead before I finished. "That all sounds good. But sorry Duggie, I don't have any cash. Can't you ask Glory?"

I told him about the catering job and the tent gig, and his face lit up.

"So they're playing this Saturday? That's great! I'll be there."

"No, you won't." I explained how it was a private party for a crowd of upper class types, etc., but when I finished he was still grinning.

"So what? I can still come. You're gonna be there right?"

"Well, of course, in my capacity as band manager I'll be there to make sure everything goes smoothly and to—"

"I'll just go with you," he interrupted. "I can carry equipment. I can be useful."

I sighed. The look of love was blazing like a five-alarm fire in his close-set eyes, and I knew better than to try to put it out. "Fine," I said. "You can come. But you have to wear nice clothes. The guests will be in formal wear. Try to blend."

"How 'bout if I just stay out of sight?"

I frowned. "How about if you just stay home?"

He grimaced. "Fine. I'll dress nice."

I considered asking him to define his terms, but I didn't feel like getting into a debate. Besides, I reflected, I hadn't given any thought to what I, as the band manager, would wear. I hadn't donned a tux since high school, and then it had been a rental. Surely something understated would suffice.

We smoked a joint and went out to meet Eric at the Tin Toad for some pizza and beer. On the way, I gave Witt the rundown on the concert plan, and he said I should get Amanda to design the flyers, so as soon as we were settled in the booth, I asked Eric if he could persuade her to do it for free.

He shook his head and said, "I'll ask her, Duggie, but I wouldn't count on it. She's really working a lot and she's kind of stressed out trying to keep up as it is." He must have seen the look on my face, because then he said, "She might know somebody else in her office who could do it. They have some interns, I think."

"Thanks," I said. Then I asked him if he could loan me a couple hundred dollars, and he said no and laughed, and I asked what was so funny and he said, "You. You seem to think we've got nothing better to do than loan you money and work for you for free."

"That's not true," I said, although I suppose I can see how he came to think that. But really? I'm a giver. It's just at the moment I'm a bit short on funds. But as soon as I get some, I'll be giving to one and all.

CHAPTER NINE

Felix qui nihil debet
Happy is he who owes nothing.

Well, the rest of the week went by faster than usual, what with Glory wearing her game face for the big doodah on Saturday, and I have to say by the time Friday came around, I was getting a bit tired of her frequent warnings and muttered threats, all along the lines of how I'd better not screw this up, etc. I took to flitting out of sight whenever she came into the room, but, of course, she had already infected me with her anxiety, even though I had complete confidence in the band. Still. It never hurts to be vigilant.

So on Friday night I drove over to the band's house to make sure they knew where to go and whatnot. I allowed Witty to ride over with me only after he agreed to my terms: speak only when spoken to and don't drool on Delilah. His eagerness was painful to behold.

"Don't worry," he assured me. "I've got to play it cool with a woman like her. I just need to give her a chance to see how I stack up next to that Tucker dude. She'll figure it out."

I was glad to note that Witty's confidence in his own appeal hadn't sustained any lasting injury from Rosalie dumping him. You would think he'd have to be used to the process by this time.

When we arrived at the house, the band seemed in a convivial mood. They didn't offer us drinks or anything, but the usual sneers and sullen stares were less frequent. I gave them the directions to the gig, and my cell phone number in case they got lost.

Delilah made Witty's night by noticing he was there.

"Who is this guy, Duggie? Does he work for you?" she asked, giving Witt a warm once-over. Luckily his face is already reddened from his honest toil in the construction field, so if he blushed no one would ever know.

"Witty's my right-hand man," I said, feeling that if I were going to lay the ground work for him, I might as well lay it thick.

"Who's your left-hand man?" quipped Crater, twirling a drum stick between his fingers.

"So what do you do?" purred Delilah, in a voice like a dish of cream.

Witty stood straighter and said, "I do whatever it takes. You got a job needs doing, I'm your man."

Tucker snorted loudly and said, "Moon, I think you're done here. Whyn't you take your monkey and leave."

Witty shot him a look that would have scorched the skin off a hot dog, but he curled his fists at his side and resisted the urge he obviously felt.

"Come on, Witt. Let's go," I said.

We left without incident and when we were driving away, I commended Witt on his self-control.

"Yeah. Well, don't count on it. That guy is askin' for it."

"That may be true. But that guy is also the lead singer, and I need him to stay healthy if the band's going to get anywhere."

"See, that's where you're wrong. That guy is nothing special. Guys like him are a dime a dozen. He thinks 'cause he's skinny and he's got the pretty boy hair and the tight pants he can play the part, but he's nothing without her. She's the one makes him look good.

She's the one makes him sound good. She doesn't need him. And neither do you."

I took a deep breath. "Whether or not that's true, and I'm not going to argue about it now, the point is, I told Glory I manage a band with six musicians, and that's what she's told these people to expect, and that's what they're going to get. So just let it go for now, okay?"

Witt scowled and stared out the window for a minute. Then he said, "I'm not gonna hurt him yet. But if he gets in my way... I can't promise anything."

Well, it wasn't exactly the calm reasoned outlook I would have preferred, but as long as the blood lust stayed off the boil, I could live with it. I had more pressing concerns, e.g. funds. I had made a list of all the possible donors, including Morris as a very last resort, but I was still hoping for a miracle of some sort. Perhaps some tipsy dowager at the party would give us a bonus, for example. Such things happen. The fact that they've never happened to me doesn't signify. Rather it might suggest that Fate has been saving up my good karma, as Phoebe would say, for this critical juncture.

The road to Darlington has so many dips and turns that by the time we arrived at the stately manor, I felt as if I had just stepped off a Tilt-a-Whirl. The ground seemed to shift beneath my feet for a few seconds. Then I took a look around and noticed with relief that the band was already there, busily setting up their equipment in the big tent behind the house. I hurried over to make sure they had everything they needed. Witty lumbered after me, looking more than a little conspicuous in the light blue tuxedo he'd rented for the occasion. I could only hope no one would laugh out loud at him. When his manhood is challenged, it takes so little to light the fuse.

But I couldn't worry about that now. Glory had caught sight of me and was charging across the lawn.

"About time you got here," she hissed. "Why aren't they starting? They're supposed to be playing cocktail music for the first hour."

"You never said anything about that."

"I certainly did." She frowned and glanced back at the patio, where a fair number of guests in party raiment were talking and drinking. "Even if I didn't, it's common sense, isn't it? You can't just start right in on "Honky Tonk Women." You've got to build up to it. Give the guests time to loosen up with some alcohol."

"They look pretty loose to me."

"Just tell the band to play some quiet instrumentals for a half hour. I'm begging you, Duggie, don't screw this up for me. These people have money up the wazoo. I'm counting on you."

Well, when she put it like that, of course, I had to agree.

"I'll see what I can do," I said. I hastened over to the band. I was pleased to note as I came closer that most of them were dressed in black, and looking reasonably presentable. Tucker was wearing tight black jeans and a black satin shirt. Delilah, in a slinky low-cut dress, had a red rose in her hair and a sparkle in her eyes. She smiled as I approached.

"Hello manager," she said. "How do we look?"

"Great," I said. "But they want some cocktail music right now. Can you guys play some soft instrumentals for a half hour?"

"You're kidding, right?" Crater came up behind me with two glasses of champagne. "We don't do soft rock," he sneered.

"Couldn't one of you just play a few standards?" I shot a glance at the keyboard guy, whose name I had yet to learn. He was a pudgy guy with a goatee and glasses. Delilah followed my gaze and nodded to him.

"Hey Denny, can you fake some lounge music?" she said.

Denny shrugged and turned a knob on the keyboard and began playing "Moon River." Oil on the waters.

Crater shook his head with a look of disgust. Then he took a sip from one of the glasses in his hands and said, "Hey, it's an open bar. You can get anything you want."

Matt nodded to Jimmy, and they set off in the direction of the bar. I watched them, wondering if I should have said something cautionary. But I didn't want to be a tyrant. After all, they only had thirty minutes. I gazed out at the crowd, which appeared to be made up of youngsters in their early twenties. They were laughing and talking loudly, paying no attention to the music. I think Glory was worried about nothing. I smiled indulgently. It would be pleasant to see her look of anxiety transformed to one of pride, once the band got going.

I turned to see where Witty had gotten to and caught sight of him chatting with Delilah at the edge of the stage. The expression on his face was so earnest and adoring, like a Labrador retriever waiting for its master to throw a stick. I had the impression that he thought he looked pretty suave in that powder blue tux. I marveled at Delilah's ability to keep a straight face.

Someone tapped me on the shoulder, interrupting my reverie. I turned and saw a girl in a yellow mini-dress perhaps a size too small for her. Her face had the glassy shine of someone feeling the effects of a couple of strong cocktails. "Hey!" she said, a bit louder than necessary I felt, inasmuch as I was standing right in front of her. "Are you with the band?"

I nodded.

"Do they know any good songs?," she asked, again with more volume than needed.

"Oh, they do," I assured her.

"Where are they?" she asked, gesturing with the hand that held her glass, which lost a bit of whatever had been in it in the process.

"Oh, they'll be right along. They're just getting started."

"Can they do 'Shout'?" she asked.

I curbed the instinct to respond with some pithy quip. It's never good form to begin by insulting the clientele. "I'll ask them," I said.

I turned to walk away and bumped into Crater. He was still carrying two glasses of champagne, and I was pleased to see that he hadn't drunk either of them yet. Such restraint boded well.

"Hey!" he said, sloshing a bit of champagne down my jacket. "When do we start?"

Eyeing him more closely, I realized that the band needed to start as soon as soon as possible. "Let me hold those for you," I said.

"S'okay," he said, and chugged the entire contents of one flute. Then he wiped his mouth with the back of his hand, gave me the empty glass, and walked toward the stage still holding the other.

I hurried over to Delilah. Before I'd said half of what I wanted, she put her hand on my sleeve and said, "Calm down, Manager. Everything's gonna be fine."

Then she gathered up the boys in the band, and they started playing some rock song I didn't recognize. But the crowd seemed to know it. They swarmed into the tent and started dancing as if their lives depended on it.

Ah, youth, I thought, sipping my ginger ale at a safe distance. Night was falling fast. The party lights strung about the lawn and garden twinkled outside the tent, which glowed like a cauldron of hormonal gumbo. Wild whoops and merry shrieks bubbled out from time to time. I caught a glimpse of Glory, bustling up near the house, and tried to catch her eye, but she was still in the thick of the action.

I, meanwhile, felt as if I'd launched my little troop to victory, and could afford a moment of well-earned respite. I'd brought along a little something just in case. I stepped into a copse of shady trees and lit the slender reefer. A couple of hits later, I returned and gazed upon the scene, and it was good.

Yet for some reason the old Latin maxim came to mind, *Plures crapula quam gladius*—more people die partying than fighting wars—which tells you something about the way those Romans used to party. In my years at UVA I minored in parties for a few semesters, and while those experiences did nothing to help my GPA, they did allow me numerous opportunities to learn from other peoples' mistakes. Thus, the ginger ale on this night, when so much depended on my ready wit and rapid response to any contingency. And, as the hours passed and the band's volume rose, I remained alert, albeit peened. Being stoned only made my senses that much more tuned to the ebb and flow of energy.

"Hey! What are you doing lurking here in the bushes? You should be out there keeping an eye on Crater, man. He's out of control." Witty focused a brooding eye on me. Then he sniffed and said, "I should have known. Man, I thought you were gonna take this seriously, Moon. Delilah's counting on you."

I took a step back. When his passions are engaged, Witt has a tendency to forget the niceties of personal space.

"Is there a problem?" I asked.

"You know Crater's drunk?"

I made a dismissive gesture. "It's a party. It's perfectly normal to have a few drinks."

"Oh yeah? How 'bout a few bottles?"

"What do you mean?"

"I mean our boy Crater decided it was too much of a pain in the ass getting his champagne in those prissy little glasses. He's been swigging from the bottles."

His use of the plural did not escape my notice. I hurried past him to the tent. It seemed a lot louder as I got closer. The tent must act as a sort of muffler. From where I'd been watching on the grassy knoll above it all, the sound level seemed festive. Here on the ground, inside the flap as it were, the din was deafening. Which might explain why everyone was shouting. That or they were all completely sloshed, which, on closer examination also appeared to be the case.

The good side of this was that in terms of client satisfaction, I'd say the band had scored a perfect ten. However, as an experienced reader of the law of diminishing returns, my trained eye told me that the party was on the brink of that tipping point, where good times can turn ugly fast. The most glaring sign of this was up on stage, where Tucker was slurring into the microphone a catalog of things he'd like to do to one of the female guests. Delilah, I noted, was watching him with a look that would have drawn blood if he'd been in range.

But in terms of sheer menace, you had to give it up for Crater, who was playing a kind of sizzling cymbal and snare drum rhythm behind Tucker. The effect was like a fighting bull snapping its tail and pawing the ground. You had the feeling no good could come of this.

And sure enough, a few seconds later Crater shot up and knocked over the brandy snifter on Matt's amplifier and it splashed onto one of the candles that were flickering all around the edge of the tent and there was a "whooosh" and suddenly a gout of flame shot up the tent wall and caught the roof on fire.

Screams followed, along with the mass exodus of stumbling revelers. I watched, more or less stunned into paralysis, fully expecting the entire place to burn to the ground. Fortunately, disaster was averted by a team of steely-eyed butlers from the main house, who appeared with extinguishers and made swift work of the fire. The party, however, was over.

As I stood surveying the soggy mess surrounding the stage, I felt a sharp poke in my side, and turned to see my sister, her makeup smeared with soot.

"You! I might have known you'd find a way to muck it up! You promised me they were civilized! Does this look civilized to you?"

I took a breath. Always a mistake.

"No. Don't bother giving me your excuses. I'm sick of them. Honestly, Duggie. Did I not tell you how important this was to me? Did you have to set fire to the tent?"

"I didn't—"

She held up her hand. I admit I flinched. She has been known to hit for lesser offenses, and, in all fairness, I suppose I had to accept partial responsibility.

"I don't want to hear a word, Duggie. You're paying for this. No matter how long it takes. I have to go up there now and try to convince them that this was all an unfortunate accident, even though we both know that's not true. You. You!" She clenched her fists and shuddered, and I could see how much it was costing her to refrain from socking me. I almost wished she would. I think she would have if there hadn't been so many people around. She always has to keep in mind the old reputation. So she just shook her head and muttered, "You'll pay for this." Then she stomped off toward the house.

I sighed. Ah well. Another day older and deeper in debt, eh? I felt suddenly tired and would have enjoyed a bit of a lie down, but I heard the band arguing at the side of the stage and realized that my work was not done.

Stepping over the broken glass and sodden debris, I edged to the side of the stage where Delilah and Matt were snarling at each other.

"You're trying to blame this on me? That's a laugh," said Matt.

"If you didn't have to have your damned brandy on the stage, none of this would have happened," said Delilah. "You might as well drink lighter fluid."

"Just because you wouldn't know the difference doesn't mean I have to drink swill like this pig." He jerked a thumb at Tucker, who was still clutching a can of light beer, which he now heaved at Matt.

Matt lunged at him and knocked him to the ground. Jimmy and Denny grabbed his arms and pulled him off. Delilah noticed me then and said, "Stop it!"

She looked at me and said, "Well, manager, how do you like us now?"

I glanced at Crater, who was sitting back behind his drums, tilting a bottle of champagne to get the last dregs past his lips. I took a long breath and caught Witty's eye. He was standing behind Delilah like a pale blue tugboat waiting to pull her away from all this.

"Well," I began, "it was going great for a while. The first two sets were outstanding." I paused. "On the down side, I think we may have to pay for the tent."

"What?" Matt, Jimmy and Denny all said this in unison. They couldn't have done it better if they'd been rehearsing.

I shrugged. "Yeah. I'm sorry too, because I was really counting on this gig to get us some momentum. But the caterer paid for the tent and they hired us and—"

"Wait a minute. Isn't the caterer your sister? She owns the Moonlight Café, right? So how come we have to pay for the tent? Doesn't she have insurance?" Delilah had her hands on her hips, and I couldn't help it, the thought just came into my head—who would win if Glory and Delilah went three rounds? I stood there, kind of seeing it in my head and then—

"Ouch!"

"Moon? I'm talking to you. Are you stoned? You are, aren't you?"

"That's neither here nor there," I began, but she interrupted again.

"That explains a lot. Maybe if you'd been paying attention, like a good manager, this wouldn't have happened. I think—" she paused and exchanged a look with the guys in the band. "I think that you should pay for the tent. And we better get paid for this gig. Because we played and we provided satisfaction. So don't think you're going to weasel out of paying us just because there was a little accident that wasn't our fault."

I opened my mouth to protest, but then I caught sight of Witty's pleading face. I could read it like it was the Sunday comics. He was begging me not to do anything that would mess up the delicate balance of the band-slash-manager relationship. And even stoned as I was, I could see his point. There has to be a certain amount of give and take in these things, just like in a marriage, I would imagine, never having been there. True, in my view, they had caused the conflagration through ill-advised actions. But if I, as manager, am charged with giving them good advice, can they be blamed if I fail to do so? I heaved a sigh. Besides, I'm a lover, not a fighter, as the fellow said. I was already in debt up to my elbows. What difference could it make if I go in up to my ears?

"Fine," I said. "I'll pay for the tent. And I'll make sure you get paid for the gig. Okay?"

Delilah smiled then, and the barometric pressure returned to normal. The moon appeared through the hole burnt in the tent. It wasn't full yet. But it always gives me a lift to see it. My namesake and all.

I trudged up to the house to see if I could convince Glory to give me the money for the band. I'd have to negotiate a payment plan for the tent. And I had no brilliant ideas for where to find the money for the hall. I couldn't even scrape up two hundred dollars for the deposit.

I was so lost in these thoughts that I wasn't paying much attention to the people mingling around the house. Though the official party was over, the after-party was just starting, and there seemed to be quite a convivial crowd in the hall between the patio and the kitchen. It was as I was trying to squirm through that I got a whiff of something powerfully familiar, and then soft lips touched my ear, and she said, "Duggie. Your band is really good."

And it was like one of those scenes where everything else freezes and there's only you and her. "You came!" I said.

"Yeah. It's funny. It turns out Miles is old friends with Leslie's parents."

"Who?"

"The girl whose birthday it is? The reason—"

"Right. The birthday girl. So did you see the—"

"Fire? Yes. It's so lucky nobody was hurt. It happened so fast!"

Her dark brown eyes were shining. She was so close. And she was wearing some kind of sexy party dress, the kind of thing she hardly ever wears when we're together. Of course, I've never taken her to a party like this. I leaned closer to kiss her, but she pulled back quickly and said, "Duggie. Miles really liked the band too. He wanted to tell you himself." She looked behind her into the crush of people. "There he is, let me get him." She pushed off, and I watched, unable to express how little I cared for whatever Miles Brandon might say to me. Unless it was to tell me he was leaving to join the Marines, solo. Then I'd wish him luck, of course. But I somehow didn't think he'd be so inclined. They don't have much use for artists in the Marines.

I had half a mind to press on in my quest to find Glory and squeeze the band's pay out of her, but before I could make any headway through the throng, Jenny was back, pinching my elbow and pulling Brandon behind her. He was looking fiendishly devil-may-care with his shirt unbuttoned halfway down to his navel and his boyish hair flopping in his eyes. Damn him.

"Fine band, Douglas. Extraordinary singer."

"You must mean Delilah," I said. No one in their right mind would call Tucker extraordinary.

"She's something. How did you find them?"

"Oh they're local talent. We have quite a lot in the county," I said, donning my managerial manner.

"I'd like to hear them again before we go. Will they be playing again soon?"

Cue ominous soundtrack. Was he trying to rub it in? Okay, Duggie, use the tools God gave you.

"Well, actually Miles, I'm working on getting a concert lined up for them in a couple of weeks. It's going to be something special. A real showcase for the band." I paused to see his reaction. As hoped, his eyes lit up.

"There're just a few logistic problems standing in the way. I was planning to use funds from this gig for the deposit to hold the hall. But now, we'll have to help cover the damage to the tent." I gave a little shrug to suggest that these things happen. What are you gonna do? "So I'm in kind of a bind."

I eyed him innocently.

He frowned slightly and asked, "How much do you need for the deposit?"

"Just two hundred dollars," I said. "Normally it would be no problem but with this..." I nodded toward the charred tent.

He glanced at Jenny and smiled. "Listen, I'd be happy to loan you the money if it means we can come see your band one more time before we leave for France."

Ouch. I felt like I'd been gaffed. He pulled out his wallet, plucked two hundred dollar bills from it, and handed them to me. And there it was, the sweet and the sour conjoined in one smarmy handful. I'd gladly let him keep his money if only he'd go to France and leave Jenny here. But that wasn't an option. So I said thanks, took the money, and went off to give Glory another chance to yell at me. Her slings and arrows would hardly register compared to this last batch of scars.

CHAPTER TEN

Fortuna sequatur
Let fortune follow.

One of the many lessons I learned during the glory days of my certamen years was that however hard you practice and study Latin verbs and Roman customs, the thin line between success or failure in competition often hinges on some trick question for which you haven't studied a whit. At that point, all that divides the conquering hero from the floundering loser is a lucky guess.

As I smoked one last joint before turning in, I tried to focus on the positive aspects of the evening. The band had been well-received, and it could even be argued that the fire that cut short the program prevented a possible slide into drunken mayhem, which, judging by Crater's disposition, seemed like a distinct possibility in the circumstances. Also on the plus side of the ledger, I now had the deposit. Reflecting on its source was a buzzkill, but *pecunia non olet*, as the fellow said. Money doesn't stink, no matter where it comes from.

On this upbeat note I was about to turn out the light when I noticed the cell phone blinking. I picked it up and discovered there was voicemail. I considered letting it wait until morning, but then I thought, what if it was good news from Jenny?

I tapped in my password, and after a stage wait Eric's voice said, "Duggie? Hey, man, I guess you're with your band, but I wanted to let you know I talked to Amanda about the flyer, and she talked to a girl in her office and she wants to meet you. Her name's Cheyenne and her number is 547-0095. You should call her soon. Amanda says she's really good at posters and stuff. So. Good luck."

I played it again so I could write down the number, and then lay back, to sleep, perchance to dream of Jenny.

By the dawn's early light, I was energetic as dammit. It was one of those brisk early October mornings when there's something in the air, the scent of burning leaves, or could be rotting leaves. Anyway, leaves. I jumped out of bed and took Rufie for a quick walk before leaving for breakfast. I had to work the brunch shift at the café, and I wanted to get the deposit up to the guy at the Hangar to hold the date. That brought me up short. I realized I hadn't actually decided on a date, and wondered if I should consult the band first. Then I considered how cranky they had been at the close of the evening before, after I told them they'd have to wait a few days to get paid, since I had to deposit the check, etc.

Reflecting on this, I decided to inform them afterward. Surely that's what a manager would do, right? Take charge. Dictate terms. I hopped in the truck and drove to the café. Glory was terse and distant throughout the shift, even though the place was packed and the kitchen was running smoothly. Eduardo has been in rare form ever since Marilyn wrapped him around her little finger, not to mention her other parts. His risottos and sauces are the stuff of legend, and the word in town is that Shipley, owner of The Black Swan, the evil empire across the street, has been writhing in torment since his efforts to lure Eduardo away failed, largely due to Marilyn. Once Glory realized that Marilyn was the key to Eduardo's happiness, she hired her to manage the bar, and the Cuban chef has been on a red-hot cooking streak. The café even got a mention in The Washingtonian a few weeks ago.

When brunch was over, I slipped away and drove out to the Hangar. The squirrelly guy who owned the place seemed surprised to see me, but he took my money, and when I asked for a receipt, he looked at me funny, but eventually produced a barely legible handwritten note, which looked less convincing than some of the notes I'd forged back in my high-school-skipping days. However, it looked legal enough for Rapidan County.

As I drove back home, I had a feeling I was forgetting something, when my cell phone burst into song, and I remembered I was supposed to call that girl. I pulled over and answered it.

"Duggie?"

"Hi."

"Did you get my message?"

"Yeah. I was just going to call her."

"Yeah. Well don't wait. She's really busy. She only agreed to do it as a favor for Amanda, and Amanda has to work with her, and she doesn't want you to piss her off."

"Who?"

"Who what?"

"Who doesn't want me to piss off whom?"

"Amanda. Amanda doesn't want you to mess things up with Cheyenne, because Cheyenne's kind of... she's really great, but she's kind of ambitious and high energy, so Amanda's a little worried that you're going to be flakey."

"I'm not now, nor have I ever been, flakey."

"Oh come on. Just don't offer her a joint, okay? She's not into that."

"Really? I would have thought if she's an artist, you know."

"Yeah. I know you. Just try to act professional. She's doing this as a favor, and when you see her work you'll understand you're really lucky."

"That's great. Tell Amanda I really appreciate it. I'll take you guys out for dinner."

"Yeah, right. Just try to be cool around Cheyenne, okay?"

"Okay. Okay."

I hung up feeling a bit peeved. Eric's known me since boyhood, so I can't expect him to worship me the way, say, Phoebe does. But he could have a little faith in me. I may have had moments of flakery in the past, but who hasn't?

I waited till I got back to the shack to make the call, so that I could project the cool professionalism of a successful band manager.

I don't know what I was expecting, but the voice that answered the phone seemed a bit... how shall I say... assertive. Female, no question, but there was definitely a touch of the big sister in her tone that made me sit up straighter.

"Cheyenne, here," she said.

"Hello, this is Doug Moon. I manage Identity Crisis."

"I don't have one."

"Um. No, I mean, that's the name of my band. The band that I manage. Amanda Carson gave me your number."

"Oh. Right. You're Duggie."

"Um. Yeah."

"And you need a flyer for a concert?"

"Yes."

"When's the concert?"

"October 30."

"Wow. Cutting it kind of close aren't you?"

"Am I? It's three weeks away."

"I'm aware. That's not a lot of time to get flyers made and distributed."

"Yes. I know it's a bit of rush."

"Can we meet today?"

"Today? It's Sunday."

There was a slight pause. "Yes. I'm aware. I'm offering to meet with you today so that we can discuss what kind of flyer you want, what type of music your band plays, what information you want on the flyer, how much you can spend—or do you want me to just guess?" There was an edge in her tone that reminded me of an algebra teacher I once had.

"No. I think it would be really good to meet. Are you in Charlottesville?"

"I live just west of Charlottesville. It shouldn't take you more than forty-five minutes to get here."

"I don't drive very fast."

"Listen. Do you want me to do this or not?"

"No. Yes. I mean, I really want you to do this and I'm happy to meet today. Can you give me directions?"

"Yes. I can," she said, and while I thought I detected a touch of impatience in her voice, it may have been my imagination. Or paranoia. Eric's warnings had unsettled me. I scribbled down the directions while she rattled them off. Luckily, I was fairly familiar with the area where she lived, so I was confident I could find it, even if it got dark before I got there, which seemed likely.

I checked my hair in the mirror and then hurried out to the truck. On the drive, I tried to imagine how the flyer should look, but honestly, art is not my best thing. I hoped Cheyenne was as good as they said.

It was completely dark by the time I arrived. I got out of the truck, looked up at the porch, and saw a portly bulldog emerge from the door. It trundled down the steps, its bark sounding like a car engine trying without success to turn over.

"That's Buster. He won't bite."

She was standing under the porch light, wearing a sports bra, biker shorts, and running shoes. As I drew near, I noticed the sheen of sweat glistening on her neck and flat stomach.

"I was working out. Come on in," she said, grabbing a towel off the bar of the fitness machine that took up half the living room.

"Do you work out?" she asked, giving me an appraising look.

"Um. Not so much."

"You should."

I stared. For the record, she was as tall as I am. She had honey-colored hair, tied up in a pony-tail, and pale blue eyes that kind of opened too wide, like she was constantly surprised. Muscles rippled down her arms and thighs, and the whole time we were standing there she was squeezing some sort of flexor device, perhaps toning up the artistic fingers.

I felt tired just looking at her.

She grabbed me by the arm, and I had the feeling she was checking the state of my muscle as she did so, and pulled me to a drafting table that stood in the corner of the room. "Pull up a chair," she said.

I did and she looked me in the eye in this sort of direct, intense way, and said, "Describe the band for me."

I must have looked confused, which, in fact, I was a bit, until she went on to say, "If you want me to create a graphic design that will get people excited enough to drive out to Dudleigh to see some band they've never heard of, I need to have some idea what they're about."

Ah. I nodded, and said, "Well, they're a six-piece rock band. Two singers, one girl, one guy. They do originals and some rhythm and blues. Umm, what more do you need to know?"

She rolled her eyes. "Well, so far you've told me nothing. There are a million rock bands that could fit that description. What makes your group stand out?"

Without hesitation I said, "Delilah."

Her expression took a turn for the better. "That should be the name of the band."

"Hmm. Maybe it could be."

"But it's not now?"

"No. They're Identity Crisis at the moment. But that could change."

"Hmm. Identity Crisis is okay. It has a sense of urgency. That's helpful."

"But you think Delilah would be better?"

She shrugged. "Delilah brings in a whole world of connections—passion, intrigue, myth, history, deception, hair—but we might as well stick with the one they're using now. If I were managing them, I'd talk to them about making a change. I assume Delilah's one of the singers?"

"Right."

"And she's hot?"

"Well, yes."

"Sultry?"

"Well, yes."

Cheyenne studied me for a minute, then she leaned over and pinched the flesh just above my belt. "I could help you with this," she said. "If you put a little effort into yourself, you could be a real boy."

I stiffened, and not in a good way. I didn't want to make her mad, but I'm happy with the way that I am. "Thanks anyway," I said. "I'm not really interested."

"Well that's just stupid," she said. "You've only got one life, one body. Why not make the most of it? You'd be amazed what a difference it could make in your life."

I fidgeted a bit. Not that I didn't appreciate her intentions, but really? I hadn't come here to be critiqued on my physique.

"Listen, umm, about the flyers—"

"Yeah. I can take care of them for you. How much were you thinking of spending?"

"As little as possible."

She frowned. "Hmm. Yeah, Amanda mentioned that you were short on cash. If you need an advance until after the concert, I know a guy with connections."

"Oh?"

"Yeah. Cliff Marshall. You may have heard of him."

I shook my head. "Not really."

"He's amazing. He's a body builder and motivational speaker. He created The Marshall Plan? His DVD changed my life."

"And you think he'd be willing to loan me money?"

"Probably not, but he knows people. He makes things happen. I'm telling you, if you want to light a fire under this band, there's nobody better than Cliff to get it going."

A spasm of caution swept over me at the word 'fire'. "Maybe I'll talk with him."

"You seriously should. I mean, you seem like a nice guy, Duggie, but you know what they say about nice guys. And if this band is counting on you to make things happen for them, you owe it to them to listen to Cliff. He's a king maker." She opened a drawer and pulled out a card and handed it to me. "Here. That's his number. I'll tell him to expect your call."

I took the card, with no intention of being bullied into something. But Cheyenne smiled at me as I pocketed it, as if I'd just taken my first step toward manhood, and although I found that irritating on a number of levels, there was a small, craven part of me that wanted her to be impressed, and I knew, somehow, that my expertise in the finer points of Latin grammar would not weigh heavily with her.

She patted me on the shoulder and said, "Okay, let's hammer out the details on these flyers, so I can have them in your hands by the end of the week. That'll give you two weeks to saturate the area."

"Great," I said. Although I wasn't feeling the greatness of it just yet. Still, I was sure it would be great once it all came together. After all, as Virgil wrote, *forsan et haec olim meminisse iuvabit*. Perhaps this will be a pleasure to look back on one day. Of course, he never managed a rock band. But the principle's the same.

CHAPTER ELEVEN

Respice finum
Look before you leap.

I hadn't really planned to meet with this guru of Cheyenne's, but after she called back a few days later and gave me an update on the flyer, including the news that it was going to cost two hundred dollars to get a thousand flyers printed the way she wanted them, I was beginning to feel a bit anxious about ye olde cash flow. So I figured it couldn't hurt to give the man a call and see whether he had any ideas for creative financing.

I punched in the number and a girl's voice answered, "Rock Solid, how can I help you?"

"Um, I'm trying to reach Cliff Marshall?"

"Let me see if he's available. Can I have your name?"

"Doug Moon."

"Hold please." The on-hold music was the theme song from "Rocky," which drummed into my ear until someone picked up the phone and said, "Doug?"

"Hi, yes. Cheyenne, um, told me to call you. She said you might—"

"Yeah, yeah. She called me. Gave me the lowdown on your situation. I can help you. We should meet. Can you come to the gym?"

"The gym?"

"My place. Rock Solid. I do all my work here. That way whenever I have any free time, I can work on my core. Or log a few k's. Keep the motor turning, you know what I'm saying?"

I blanched. I have nothing against fitness freaks. It takes all kinds and whatnot. I've heard people gush about endorphins and all of that. But for me, the specter of the gym rekindles some of my least pleasant memories of high school, when illiterate jocks considered a day wasted if it didn't include some form of torture-the-geek.

"I guess I can come there, if that's what it takes."

There was a slight pause on the line, and then he said, "Moon? Cheyenne told me you're lookin' to borrow some money. That right?"

"Um, yes. Just a short term loan for—"

"Yeah, I don't care what it's for," he interrupted. "Here's the thing, Moon. If you want something, you got to be willing to do whatever it takes—whatever it takes, you understand? Now, if you don't really need my help, well, then I got better things to do. Best of luck to you."

"No, I... I really do need some help, I'm just... when do you want to meet?"

"I could see you today between three and four. That work for you?"

"Yeah. That'll be great. I'll be there."

"Rock on." He hung up, and I was alone with my thoughts.

On the long drive up Route 29, and then the considerably less scenic segment of Route 66, I had lots of time to reflect on the wisdom of borrowing money from persons unknown. But the more I considered my options, the more I realized I didn't have any. I'd already touched everyone I knew who actually had money, and there was no bank in the world that would consider me a good risk. That's one of the downsides to abandoning the white collar work force in favor of the honest toil of a dishwasher/busboy in my sister's restaurant. On the plus side, my needs were few, living in my modest shack, and I had mastered the art of living within my means. *Nec habeo, nec carea, nec curo*: I have not, I want not, I care not. I haven't been in debt since I paid off my college loans, and I wasn't eager to take on a new burden, but I comforted myself with the conviction that this loan was simply a temporary measure to get my career as a band manager off to a flying start. Once this concert was over, I'd be on my way.

The traffic getting to Springfield was slow, but at least it kept moving. I drove past the place before I saw it. Once I did, I couldn't believe I'd missed it the first time. It was sandwiched between a dry cleaner and a pizza carryout in a shabby strip mall, but what arrested the eye was a sort of faux mountain peak, jutting up out of the flat roofline. Glaring neon letters going up the side of the edifice spelled out the word, "Ascend." At the top, a flag fluttered with the words "The Marshall Method."

I parked and went inside. A pretty girl in a spandex bodysuit was behind the desk. The atmosphere was charged with the clang of weights and the grunts of strong men. The hum of treadmills thudded in the distance. The girl looked at me, and I said, "I'm here to see Cliff Marshall?"

"And you are?"

"Doug Moon."

"Moon. Right on time. Good job." A tall guy in shorts with a shaved head and massive biceps came toward me with his hand out. I took it hoping he wouldn't crush my fingers. He gave a quick pump and let go, then stepped back and looked me up and down.

"You don't work out, do ya?" he said.

I bristled inwardly. I didn't ask him if he read Cicero, did I? But I stifled my ready wit and muttered something about lack of time.

He shook his head in a pitying way. "Moon, one thing you've got to recognize. There's always time to do the important things. You just have to learn what they are. Workin' out's like breathin'. You gotta do it." He put a hand on my shoulder and led me through a doorway. "Come on. You came here for a reason. Let's deal with that first. Tell me what you need."

I went into my spiel about the concert, the cost of renting the hall, the flyers, the porta-johns, the lights, etc. I was going to touch on the burnt tent, but I didn't want him to get the idea the band was irresponsible, so I left that out.

"So bottom line, what's the number?"

"Um...?"

"How much do you need? When do you need it? When will you be able to pay it off? This is what my associates need to know. They're businessmen."

Well, of course I did have a number in mind. I felt a little awkward about naming it, but I managed to say, "Two thousand."

He didn't bat an eye. "You sure that's enough? It's better to get more than you need than to underestimate and fall short. It's like a fight. Always better to over prepare than under prepare."

I considered this. He was right, of course. Two thousand was the bare minimum, when you considered I'd probably have to hire people to distribute the flyers, run the sound system, and so on. "Maybe you're right. Can I make it three thousand? Just to be sure?"

"It's your call, buddy. This band, you're their manager?"

"Yes."

"And they're counting on you?"

"Yes."

He shook his head. "When people are counting on you, you can't let 'em down. Am I right?" He held a hand up in the high-five position.

"Right," I said, and slapped his hand with mine. I didn't see what else I could do.

"Do I need to sign anything?" I asked, as an afterthought.

He grinned and said, "Nah. These guys I work with, they're not big on paper work. They got a code of their own. They do their part. You do yours. Everybody wins."

I nodded. "That sounds great. Um..."

He smiled at me again. "You wanna know when you get the dough?"

"Um, yes."

"Do you need some right away?"

"Actually, I could use a few hundred right away."

He nodded. "No problem. I can front you that until the brothers get the rest of it to you. Where can they find you?"

I hesitated. "Oh. They'll come to me?"

Cliff chuckled as if at a private joke. "Oh yeah. They like to know where all their clients live. It simplifies things. Give your address to Marlene at the desk, we'll take care of the rest." He put an arm across my shoulders. It felt as if someone had draped me with a sheep. "You're making a smart move," he said. "We'll get you shaped up in no time."

I nodded weakly and went out, after giving Marlene my address. Actually I gave her the address of the café, because that's where I get my mail. I don't technically have an address at the shack. One of the perks of being off the grid. I didn't mention that to Cliff because I had a feeling he wouldn't understand. There are some people you just know never get high. Although, I guess he's got his own up trip, hah. Ascend. Phew. Not in a million years, Cliffy.

It was with a feeling of some relief that I sat in the rush hour sludge on Route 66 heading home. My feeling of well-being lasted until I got to Centreville, when I happened to turn on the radio and heard that it was almost five o'clock. I was supposed to be at the café already. Glory would be incandescent. I suppose I could have called her right then to decant some of the lecture. But then I thought, why spoil the moment? The sun was a perfect red ball sinking over the

Blue Ridge in the distance. I was on my way back to the mountains. Life's petty irritants slipped from my mind like so much dross. I was headed for a better kind of glory.

The next day, when I showed up for the lunch shift, Glory greeted me with a slap on the back and cheery hello, and I confess I was a bit surprised at the rapid turnaround from her cold wrath of the previous evening. I had expected that it would take weeks of contrition and kowtowing to restore her mood. With anyone else I might have suspected a new love interest as the cause, but since her divorce Glory has more or less given up on men. Her only love is her business, which is why the recent tent fiasco hit the tender spot.

"You seem in a good mood," I said, digging for details.

"No thanks to you," she snapped.

Ah, that's more like it. Back to normal.

"Well, I'm glad to see it anyway," I said, and I meant it. She's a lot easier to be around when she's not ticked off.

"You want to know why, don't you?" she said. She knows me too well.

"I'm just glad you aren't mad at me anymore."

"Who said I wasn't?"

Right. I sighed and started for the kitchen.

"Dugger."

She's the only person in the world who uses this term, and its use generally implies a softening of the sisterly death grip. I turned and gave her a raised eyebrow.

"I suppose you have a right to know that something good came out of that debacle Saturday."

"It did?"

"I got a call yesterday from the woman who hired me, and she went on and on about how good the food was and how much her guests enjoyed the party."

"And the fire?"

"She didn't even mention it. She asked me if I could get in touch with your piano player. Apparently she's friends with the Claytons. They own a winery just outside of Darlington, and they're having a wine tasting this Saturday. They were at the party, and they liked the cocktail music. They want to hire your piano player, and maybe the girl singer, to play for their event. They offered to pay them two hundred dollars to play for three hours. I said I'd tell you about it. Here's their number." She handed me a card.

"Thanks," I said.

She smiled and patted me on the back. "You might suggest that they try not to burn the place down."

"Right."

Well, who knew? I wasn't sure how the band would feel about this, but I decided to call Delilah and lay it out for her. If she didn't like the idea, they could turn it down.

When my shift was over, I went out to the parking lot and made the call. After I'd given her the basic outline, Delilah fell silent for a minute, and I didn't know whether to keep talking or if she'd hung up.

"So, this two hundred dollars... that would be for just me and Dennis?"

"Right."

"I don't know a lot of lounge music."

"You probably know more than you think. Isn't it mostly old show tunes and stuff? It's not like a concert or something. You guys will be background music."

"Huh." She fell silent again for a few seconds. Then she said, "What the hell, I could use the money. We'll do it."

"Great. I'll get the directions and stuff and swing by later."

"You can call."

"Okay... I just thought—"

"Yeah. You're a thinker. It might be better of you stayed away for a while. Some of the guys weren't too happy after Saturday."

"Oh."

"Don't worry. They'll get over it. Just give 'em some time."

"They still want to do the concert though, right?"

"The concert?"

"The big concert I'm putting on for you at the Hangar. I told you—"

"Oh right, sure. Halloween, right? Yeah. We're doing that. But call me with the deal on this wine thing. I'll brush up on my Dionne Warwick."

I hung up, feeling a little deflated. These musician types were so much touchier than I'd imagined they'd be. Luckily I'm experienced with situations that require finesse. It's like Hearts. You have to know how to play the hand you're dealt.

Glory let me off early that night, and I was glad of it. I got back to the shack around eight, looking forward to a few carefree hours with my guitar. But no sooner had I cracked open a beer and rolled a thin reefer, than I heard Rufie barking outside. I tiptoed to the window. Ever since Sheriff Quayle put me on his to-do list, my paranoia has never really gotten the kind of rest a good neurosis needs.

The car out front was unfamiliar, but when a statuesque honey-blonde woman stepped out of it, even in the October darkness I recognized Cheyenne whatever-her-last-name-was. What was she doing here? And how did she find me?

I stashed the joint in a drawer and hastened to the door, opening it just before she knocked.

"Hi," she said. "Can I come in?" She was holding a big cardboard box.

"Of course. Um, was I expecting you? I mean, did we...?"

"I just got the flyers back from the printers, and I thought you'd like to see them. They turned out great." She stepped inside and glanced around my little shack. It's basically one room, so it doesn't take long.

"Cute place. Here," she said, putting the box on the table and pulling out a flyer. "What do you think?"

The flyer exploded on my retina like a ripe tomato. It was all hot-cherry-pink and electric-lime with black lettering in a style reminiscent of the hallucinogenic sixties. Sort of like a car wreck. You couldn't look away.

"Wow." I stared at it, feeling my pupils dilate. "That's really... something."

"Yeah, I know. It's a traffic stopper. I could have gone quieter, but since your time is so short, you really need to grab people fast and hold them."

"Yeah," I said, blinking. "It's really... bright."

She gave me a quick look. "There's a lot of competition in the flyer trade, Moon. Pastels don't cut it. You have to shock people into looking. You want the design to imprint on their memory banks. Then you've got them."

I nodded. I had to assume she knew what she was doing. I knew I'd never be able to forget the image, which seemed to be of a distraught person of indefinite gender pulling his or her hair out.

"He's in crisis, see?" she said, pointing to the question marks flying out like sparks from his head.

"Yeah. I get it."

She frowned. "Trust me. This is going to get their attention. It'll bring in the fans."

I swallowed, feeling a bit like I'd just dropped a tab of acid. Too late to worry now. I turned to her and managed a smile. "They look great." And then I noticed, looking at her, that though she wasn't wearing her sports bra and shorts, she was dressed in a way that seemed to suggest a motivation of a different kind. She wore a halter top that only just covered the facts, so to speak, and her hair was all fluffed out around her face, kind of Farrah-style, and her hips curved in a tight leather mini-skirt. Most alarming of all, there was a gleam in her eye, like that of a tiger sizing up a gazelle.

I took a step back warily, putting the table between us. She laughed, as if I'd done something amusing. I started talking, fast.

"Well, I was really surprised to see you drive up. Not many people know where I live. How did you find me?"

She chuckled again. She was slowly edging around the table to my side. I cagily edged the other way.

"Eric gave me directions. He comes over to meet Amanda after work, you know? He told me you've been lonely since your old girlfriend left." She lowered her chin and gave me a look.

"Really? He said that? I don't know where he gets his information. My girlfriend, Jenny, hasn't left me. She's just got a new job, and she's working a lot more than she used to. That's all. You know she's Amanda's sister?"

Cheyenne took another step toward me. "Yeah. I talk with Amanda all the time. She's really sweet. She told me your girlfriend's leaving you to go to France. With her hot boss."

Her claws left a mark with that one. I forgot what I was doing for a moment, and she closed the distance between us. She had doused herself with some powerful perfume, and at close range it was nearly suffocating. I gasped slightly and said, "Amanda and Eric don't understand about Jenny and me. What we have... our relationship is deep. Miles deep."

She didn't appear to be paying any attention to what I was saying. She ran a hand up my arm until her fingers rested on my neck. I started sweating.

"Relax, Moonie. I'm not gonna hurt you," she whispered. She pinched my bicep, and again I had that feeling of being measured and found wanting. "You can't go through life being afraid. You'll miss all the fun." She blew in my ear as she said this, and I jumped slightly to get away. She laughed again and closed her eyes halfway, and said, "I'm not gonna bite you. At least not until we build you up a little so you can bite back."

I was trying to appear nonchalant. I'm not sure she got it. But at least she stopped her advances and gave me another look. I had no idea what it was supposed to convey, but, thankfully, she seemed to lose interest in me for the moment. She sort of sniffed and went to the door. When she reached it, she turned her head toward me and said, "Good luck with the flyers. If you need anything else, call me. I'll be waiting."

And on that note, she sashayed out into the night. I sank to the floor trembling with relief, feeling as if a life-threatening boulder had just crashed down a mountainside and bounced across the road in front of my car, narrowly missing me.

I mean, I've had female admirers in the past. Not a lot. Not like Alvin. However, in the days when my certamen medals were newly minted, there were more than a few dewy-eyed girls who followed my every move. But even then, no one like Cheyenne had ever taken note of my existence, and I was somewhat baffled as to what she saw in me. It occurred to me that she might be one of those "molding" type of females, never happier than when working on some project, in this case me, with the goal of building a better boyfriend. I shuddered.

Needless to say, I have no desire to be improved for anyone's sake but Jenny's, and she likes me just the way I am. So. The trouble is, I'm not suited to these fiery high-octane girls. All my talking points—my sly wit, my dry humor and genial charm—fall flat in the presence of women who admire the sort of square-jawed, steely-eyed sons of the soil whose idea of a good time runs along the lines of hand-to-hand combat.

But—and here was the sticking point—I couldn't just push Cheyenne gently toward the exits, because I couldn't afford to piss her off, not only because her skills were tied up with the success of the flyers and thus the success of the concert and the whole win-Jenny-back program, but also because her happiness, Cheyenne's that is, had a direct impact on Amanda's as a result of their working closely together, and Amanda's happiness was vital to Jenny's. You see? The foundation of the House of Moon would collapse if I failed to keep this Cheyenne whatever-her-last-name-was in my corner.

It was the sort of prickly predicament that normally would have sent me running to Morris for advice. But, what with him turning his back on me and my blues playing, the pride of the Moons wouldn't allow me to go crawling back for advice.

I mused on this for a while, before I remembered what I'd been about to do when Cheyenne's arrival threw me off. I went to the drawer, fired up the reefer, and within a short time had regained the calm, reflective attitude that is my natural state. The joint helped, of course. The philosopher's stone is my best thing. Ask anyone.

CHAPTER TWELVE

Quod cito acquiritur cito perit
Easy come, easy go.

The next morning I got up early and drove to Charlottesville. At the UVA student union building, I found a couple of needy undergrads, who agreed to distribute the flyers all around town for a flat fee. I was almost getting used to throwing money out the window, and when the pair demanded fifty bucks apiece to blanket the area, I didn't even blink. It was all starting to feel like Monopoly money to me.

I made it back to Dudleigh in time to work the big Friday lunch crowd, and after the last dish was loaded up in the washer, Glory asked me if anything had come of the winery gig. When I told her they were going to do it, she asked if I was going to be there.

"I hadn't planned on it. Why? Do you think I should be?"

"No. Not necessarily. If it was me, I'd be there. But, you're you," she grimaced a bit as she said this, but from her that's almost like getting a gold star.

"Oh, I know why I was asking," she continued. "Your friend Morris was at the café this morning. I bumped into him, and he asked me how things went with your band. I was surprised you hadn't been filling him in on every little detail. I thought he was like your shrink."

I flared the nostrils a bit, by way of letting her know she was on thin ice. "Morris and I are on a break," I said.

"Really? How come?"

"It's nothing really. Just one of those things."

"Oh. Well, I told him about the winery job. He seemed interested. That's why I was asking if your band was going to be there. Or you."

"Ah. Well, if Morris is going that's another reason for me to give it a miss."

"Aw. You should kiss and make up. It's good for you to have at least one intelligent friend."

"Thanks. I'll consider it."

I pushed off. Though I had led her to believe this rift with Morris was a mere nothing, the truth was I really wished I could bend his ear about the various angles of this managerial role. There was so much more to it than I'd originally thought. HarLar had made it sound like a walk in the park, but I was beginning to sense that this particular park was one of those where the winos sleeping under the benches aren't the worst you have to fear.

Also, it being the second Friday of the month, our traditional night for the Hearts league, I was not looking forward to hosting the event in my cramped quarters. The shack is perfect for one man, and, ideally, one woman, but add three beer-drinking pals, and the place starts to feel a bit congested. That's why we usually invade Morris's spacious home, where he puts up with us, because he likes to smoke our pot. But in the current standoff, I didn't see how I could just descend on him as if nothing had changed. It was sort of sad. Ironically, it gave me an idea for a blues song.

Later, once Witty and Eric and Randall were leaning back in their chairs and drinking their second beers while I dealt, I gazed around at our tight little group and felt the tension lifting from my soul. Here

I was, surrounded by my pals, pleasantly buzzed, and in the lead after two hands. Life was good. I didn't need Morris.

"Hey Duggie, what's this I hear about you puttin' on a concert at the Hangar?" Randall was arranging his cards, considering his pass.

"It's gonna be great. On Halloween," I said, passing three cards to Witty.

Witt frowned as he looked at them. "That place is a dump," he said.

"Yeah. It's a hole. What's wrong with the firehouse?" Randall asked.

I sighed. People outside the business naturally can't comprehend the amount of thought that goes into these decisions. "The Hangar can hold six hundred people. I need to get a big crowd because I've got to make some money. Plus, the firehouse was already booked, as was every other hall within a hundred miles."

"Wow. I guess Halloween's a big night for parties. You're going to have a lot of competition for your audience," said Eric, slipping three cards to me.

I picked them up and scowled at the sight of the king of spades and two worthless mid-range diamonds. I wasn't really bothered by the cards so much as the fact that Eric had actually raised an issue, which I had been attempting to ignore, ostrich-like. Halloween is a huge party night, and there would be tons of choices for those seeking diversion. I had to hope those flyers worked their magic. It had occurred to me that the lazy, college crowd might be disinclined to drive forty-five minutes out of town, when they had options within stumbling range.

As the quiet snap and shuffle of the cards filled in the silences, I tried to put my fears to rest, but of course, everyone else kept waking them up again.

"I don't get it, Duggie. Why're you doin' this anyway? Yer never gonna get rich skimmin' ten percent off the top of a band that's goin' nowhere." Randall gathered up the cards, as it was his turn to shuffle.

"I'm not trying to get rich. I just want to show Jenny that there's more to me than... it seems."

Eric looked over at Randall and said, "Jenny's working for a good-looking rich guy, who's also a successful artist, who's taking her to France in a couple of weeks."

"Whoa," said Randall. He looked at me and shook his head. "And you think managing some rinky-dink band is gonna beat that?"

I sighed. I had hoped to avoid thinking about this painful subject for a few carefree hours, but apparently this was not to be. "My plan is that Jenny will come to the concert, and it will be so great that she'll remember what it is she loves about living here, and she'll realize she's going to miss out on all the good times ahead if she goes to France."

"Hunh." Randall finished dealing and picked up his cards with a shake of his head. "Well, this hand don't look too good, but compared to yours, it's a straight flush."

"We're not playing poker," I said,

"Good thing too, or you saps would be owing me big time," said Witty. He took a sip from his beer, and after a few minutes said, "You know what I don't get?"

"What?" said Randall.

"What is it with women and France? Seems like they all have this thing, you know? Like Paris? What's the deal? Every chick I meet wants to go there. Why is that? Maybe they got the lock on pastries, but name one rocker who ever came out of France. You can't do it. There aren't any. Their music is for shit. And you go over there, what are you gonna do?"

"Bring your own," said Eric, dropping the queen of spades on the table.

"Aw shit," said Witty. "Go ahead, pile 'em on. This ain't my night."

As we counted up the points, Witty clunked down his empty beer bottle on the table and said, "Delilah's not like that. She doesn't care about France. She's got a rock and roll heart."

Eric and Randall and I all looked at him and exchanged a mute glance. None of us was foolish enough to touch this tempting bon mot. Witty had more muscle than all three of us combined.

As he was dealing the next round Eric said, "You know, Duggie, even if I don't agree with Randall about the managing a band thing, I think it's good you're trying something new. I think you ought to try to... maybe move on."

"What are you talking about?" I said.

"You know. From Jenny. Everybody knows you've carried the torch for her since high school, but it seems like this thing with Brandon is for real and... you know, maybe you need to move on."

I glared at him. Eric, of all people, whose hopeless love for Jenny's sister I had fully supported, and now here he was telling me to give up.

"I just want you to be happy, man. And Jenny's leaving. You gotta accept it." He looked at me as if I were the crazy one.

"No, I don't," I said.

"You know Cheyenne really likes you."

"Hah!" I shuddered slightly. "Not a chance in hell, do you hear me? I'll be polite for Amanda's sake, but if you think I'm going down that road, you are waaaay wrong."

"Who's Cheyenne?" Witty asked.

"She's a graphic artist. She works in the same office with Amanda," said Eric.

"And...?" I prodded. I didn't want to be the one to point out the woman's flaws, but I couldn't believe Eric was blind to them.

"And what?" Witty asked, looking from me to Eric.

I raised my eyebrows at Eric.

"She's a little, um, high energy," he said.

"That's one way of putting it," I said.

"Hey, what's wrong with energy?" Randall asked. "Unless she's pushy." He glanced at me and I rolled my eyes. "Oh." he said. Then he shrugged and looked at Eric. "Hey man, nobody wants a pushy woman."

Eric pretended to be concentrating on his cards, but I knew he couldn't argue the point.

Witty snapped a card on the table and said, "There's nothin' wrong with a woman being strong. Kinda sexy, I think."

"Oh yeah? Let me give you Cheyenne's number," I said.

Witty grimaced at me. "You know I'm committed."

"I know you ought to be."

"Yeah, that's funny. No wonder your girlfriend left you."

"Hey!" said Eric. "Let's not talk about women, okay? We're here to play cards."

"Right on," said Randall, who never has woman problems. He seems to change girlfriends with the seasons without any great histrionics or emotional jetlag. Easygoing should be his middle name.

We played in silence for a few hands, then Eric said, "You know, what you ought to do at the Hangar is put up some decorations. Halloween stuff. Give it some atmosphere."

"That's not a bad idea, but I'd need to get someone else to do it. It's not my thing. And I'm already spending a fortune."

"I didn't know you had one," quipped Randall.

"I don't. I've been borrowing money like crazy." I frowned slightly. The thing was, it was a good idea. If I could get someone to do it for free. I looked at Eric. "Do you think Amanda—"

"Forget it. Every time you want something, you try to get her to work for you for free. There's no way. She's so stressed out at her job already, I have to be in full support mode every time we're together."

Randall frowned. "What does that mean?"

"I listen while she vents, and hand her tissues when she cries."

"Sheesh. If my woman did that, it'd be time to trade-in for a new model."

Eric clammed up then, but I could tell he was fuming in his quiet way. He doesn't like arguing, especially with someone like Randall, who enjoys fighting of any kind.

It was getting late, and we had called the last round, when Rufie went bounding to the door, wagging his tail.

"Did someone just drive up?" Eric asked.

I cringed, hoping that it wasn't Cheyenne. But then I told myself that Rufie only wags that way when it's someone he likes, and a minute later this proved to be the case.

"Who's a big boy? Who's a good Rufie?" I hadn't heard Phoebe's voice in a while, but the sound of it triggered an inspiration. I seemed to recall that she had a way with crepe paper and glitter and whatnot during certamen festivities.

"Hey, am I interrupting your game?" she asked as she came in.

"No, not at all. We just played the last hand," I said.

"Perfect timing," said Randall, eyeing Phoebe with approval.

Being a few years younger than the rest of us, Phoebe still exudes a kind of nymphet air, and her attire leans toward the bright and spangly style of the cheerleader she once was, which enhances the effect. Even Eric found it hard to look away.

I, on the other hand, was all business. "So Phoebes, what brings you here at this hour? Not that I'm not always glad to see you." I was working my way into it, you see, before I began to play on her natural affection for me to get her to do my bidding.

She pulled a bright piece of paper from behind her back and said, "This!"

The flyer glowed like some toxic, post-apocalyptic artifact.

"Jeez," said Randall, shielding his eyes.

"They're awesome!" said Phoebe, bouncing with enthusiasm. Just looking at her made me feel that everything was going to be all right.

"You like it?" I asked.

113

"They're great! And they're everywhere. I got this one at Dojo Doughnuts. I can't wait. I love Halloween parties. This is such a great idea, Duggie."

Well, some say that too much praise is bad for you, but I suspect those are losers who never experienced it. Trust me, you never tire of praise.

"You know, Phoebes, Eric and I were just talking about how what would make this concert the best ever would be some Halloween decorations, and I'm not good with that sort of thing, but as I recall, you are. Do you think there's any way—"

Her face lit up like a handful of sparklers. "Oh Duggie! I would love to do the decorations!" The sparklers fizzled. "But... the Hangar's really huge isn't it? It will take a lot of stuff to dress it up right." Her forehead puckered in thought and she made what was, for her, a serious expression. Picture a squirrel pondering where it hid the peanut. I waited silently, hoping her natural resilience would have her back at the top of the pyramid in a few minutes, and sure enough, as Witt and Randall were heading out the door, she came to life and said, "Parachutes!"

Well, okay. Eric and I exchanged a look and a shrug and waited for more.

"That's the answer," she explained. "We can get some orange parachutes and drape them from the ceiling and rig lights behind them, so they'll look like giant pumpkins. The rest will be easy. Some skeletons, cobwebs, cauldrons with dry ice. It'll be amazing!"

I smiled. Ah. Another crisis averted.

"I'll need some money," she said. "You know, I'll try to get stuff for free, but I'll have to pay for some of it."

Right. More money. Of course.

"No problem," I said. "It'll be worth it."

After they had all gone, I sat out on the porch, listening to the crickets and enjoying the crisp scent of October. Orson, perhaps sensing I was in a receptive mood, jumped onto my lap, and I let him stay, even though he weighs a ton, possibly from bingeing on crickets. Things were falling into place with the band and the concert. I was hopeful. I imagined Jenny walking into the Hangar on Halloween and being dazzled by the lights, the music, and me. She'd see that she couldn't leave, then. It would be obvious. It had to be.

CHAPTER THIRTEEN

Non semper erit aesta
It will not always be summer.

Have you ever noticed how, no matter where they live, people complain about the weather? I mean, I've never been to Tahiti, so I couldn't say for sure whether or not they have climate issues even in paradise, but here in Virginia, there's no shortage of material for those who enjoy a good weather rant. The heat, the humidity, the freezing cold, ice 'events', torrential rains. We get it all. But for those of us who choose to stay here for whatever reason, the payoff comes in the fall, when the very air seems distilled to its finest essence—clearer, brighter, more alive. Some people rave about the autumns of New England or New York, and those may have their charms, but for me, nothing beats fall in Virginia. Crisp apples, cloudless skies, and the Blue Ridge turned to gold.

The only downside to this picture is that each year the D.C. weather forecasters make a sport of charting the progress of the autumnal color, predicting the peak weekend for taking in the fall colors. Thus, the regular heavy weekend traffic becomes bloated to the point of madness by the influx of Leafers, day trippers who come to sip the wine and admire the views.

For Glory this season is like the running of the salmon in the Pacific Northwest. She counts on reeling in the famished hordes and relieving them of their disposable income (she's recently added a line of Moonlight Café souvenir t-shirts, coffee mugs and the like, and sales have been brisk she tells me). So, it was with a sinking heart that I pulled in for my double shift on Saturday. The lot was already packed.

The atmosphere in the kitchen was like a beach town when a hurricane is expected for dinner. A bit tense and brooding. Eduardo, never exactly a sunny personality, had his game face on. The sous chefs were darting quickly between the counters, stirring, chopping, mashing. I slipped past them to the relative calm of the sinks, where a tower of dirty dishes and pots awaited. From that point on I never got a break, even after the lunch hour officially ended, because when the Leafers get hungry you have to feed them well, so they don't go home and bad mouth the café. I got a ten minute break sometime around four, just long enough to smoke half the joint I'd brought along.

It was almost ten, as I pushed the button on the last dishwasher load, when I realized that I had totally forgotten about the winery gig. I had hoped to drop by between the lunch and dinner shifts and see how it was going. Oh well. Presumably Delilah and Denny had satisfied the customers. I was too tired to worry about it.

The next day it was more of the same. Brunch lasted until almost five o'clock. I was glad I'd embarked on a new career. I don't want to be washing dishes when I'm forty.

I think Glory must have seen something in my expression, because she let me go home before the dinner shift. I fell onto the bed when I got there, planning to rest just a few minutes before taking Rufie for a run. But I guess I must have passed out, because the next thing I knew I felt a soft touch on my shoulder and heard a voice saying, "Duggie?"

I'd been dreaming of this moment so often that at first I thought it was just another one of those. I reached out to pull her closer, figuring, what the hell, make the most of it. But she sort of smiled and shook her head. That's when I knew it wasn't a dream.

"We need to talk," she said. Are there any four words more foreboding?

I sat up and stared at her. She looked amazing of course. Her hair was tumbling all loose around her shoulders, the way I like it. And she was wearing some kind of sweater that... she was talking. I missed something.

"What? I'm sorry. I didn't..." I shook my head to clear it. "Okay. What's up?"

She looked at me with those big brown eyes, and I could see something bad coming. "Are you hungry?" I said, talking fast. "Or some tea? Coffee? I might have a beer in there."

She shook her head in this sad kind of way. I could see this wasn't easy for her. That was something, at least. She must still care about me. A little.

"Duggie, you know how I feel about you."

"I think so."

"You mean a lot to me. You always have. You always will. But..." She swallowed, and I took a deep breath. Here it comes.

"The thing is, Miles is different from anyone I've ever known. He's a man of the world. I know that's a cliché, but it's true with him. He knows so much, and he's so generous... to me. He wants to give me things—not that I care about things, you know? But... I'm not saying this very well." She reached out and put her hand on my arm. I wanted her to stop. To say, just kidding, and laugh and punch me, and then we'd kiss and... But that wasn't happening. I felt kind of sick to my stomach.

She went on, talking about how much Miles respected her, and how he'd told her that she was wasting her life working as a waitress out here, and that she could do better than me. And, of course, all of that's true. But, so what? I love Jenny, and she loves me. I know she does. And I'm trying to be a better man for her and—

"Duggie? Are you listening? You look like you're miles away."

I snorted. The word "miles" has a new sting.

"Yeah. I'm listening. I know you deserve a better man. I just don't think he's the one."

"You don't know him."

"Do you?"

She stiffened just a little. Then she sighed and said, "I know this is hard for you. It's hard for me. And I don't know if it's going to work out with Miles, but I feel like I need to take this chance to see more of the world. Maybe find a new career. Can you understand that?"

I hung my head. Of course I understood it. I just hated it, that's all.

So naturally I nodded and told her that I would always love her and that I wanted her to be happy. She smiled then and hugged me, and then she left.

I sat there while the room grew dark, until Rufie came over and put his paw on my knee. "Yeah, I know, pal," I said. "Let's go."

We walked around the woods behind the shack. Rufie crashed through the leaves, happy to be alive. I was glad one of us was.

When we came back to the shack, it was so dark and cold that I didn't have the heart to go in and spend the evening with my thoughts. Even the idea of playing the blues seemed too bleak. I glanced up the trail to Morris's house and wondered if he was home and if he'd be willing to lend an ear. I even missed his sarcasm.

I started up the path. Rufie bounded happily ahead. He likes Morris.

There were lights on at the house and some kind of jazz playing on the stereo. I knocked on the door, and he opened it with a look of mild surprise.

"Did you sell your guitar?"

"No. But... can we talk?"

He shrugged and opened the door wider. Rufie stayed on the porch. I went in and sat by the wood stove. It was cozy.

Morris sat in his big leather chair and looked at me with that "the Buddha will see you now" expression. Sometimes that irks me, but right now, in my emotionally bruised state, I actually smiled to see him there, looking all professorial. Even a know-it-all can have moments of charm.

At first I didn't know where to begin, but when I opened my mouth it just came out. "I'm afraid Jenny's leaving me."

"Can you blame her?"

I frowned. So predictable. "That's not the point."

"What is?"

"I don't want to lose her. She's the best thing in my life."

He looked at me for a few seconds and then said, "You must not be the best thing in hers."

"Thanks a lot."

"You brought it up."

"I thought you might have some advice for how to keep her."

"You might try getting a real job."

I rolled my eyes. "I'm working on that."

He raised his eyebrows.

"The band? My new career as a manager?"

"How's that working out? I think I saw your singer yesterday."

"Delilah?"

"Is that her name? How apt."

"Where'd you see her?"

"I went to a wine tasting near Darlington. Some friends have a vineyard there. She was singing. There was a piano player. They didn't seem quite at home with the material."

"What do you mean?"

He shrugged. "She was reading the lyrics, and she didn't seem familiar with them."

"Are you saying they were bad?"

"No. They were decent. Just not as smooth as those type of musicians usually are." He looked at the stove for a few seconds. "She's something, though. I'll give you that. She's definitely got animal magnetism."

"Huh. Well, she's more of a rock and roller. If you heard her with the band you'd appreciate it more."

"I didn't say I didn't appreciate it. It was entertaining. I think the people there liked it."

"Well that's all that matters."

A minute of silence passed, and I wondered briefly if he was waiting for me to pull out a reefer, since usually he depends on me to get him stoned. I felt in my pockets and came upon a skinny emergency joint that I'd forgotten about. I pulled it out and held it up. He made a 'be my guest' gesture, so I lit it up and passed it to him. He kept it for a while.

When he finally passed it back, he said, "How are things going with your little band, anyway? I heard they set fire to a tent in Darlington."

"Oh really? Who told you about that?"

"That sculptor fellow, the one who's stealing your woman. Brandon? He was there, sampling the wine. I overheard him telling some people about the conflagration. He got a big laugh."

"He would."

"He can't help it if he's good looking, rich and amusing."

"That doesn't give him the right to take Jenny away."

"Perhaps not. But as Virgil said, *possunt quia posse videntur*. He can because he thinks he can."

Not many people can go toe-to-toe with me on Latin quotations. But I couldn't argue this one. Damn this Brandon. Why couldn't he have the good grace to have a fatal flaw? A huge nose, say. Or rank body odor. I wasn't picky. Any little completely off-putting trait would do.

If I'd hoped that Morris would provide a brilliant suggestion for how to win Jenny back, and let's face it, that's what I really want, he failed to deliver. But before I left, he said he'd give it some thought, so I'm still hopeful that he may come up with something. I felt a little better after talking to him anyway. Being smart is good for everyday use, but when the going gets tough, it's good to have a friend who's even smarter than you are.

CHAPTER FOURTEEN

Stat nulla diu mortalibus usquam, fortuna titubante, fides
Men do not remain loyal for long where Fortune proves unstable.

I waited until noon to head over to the band's house. I didn't want to get there while they were still sleeping off the weekend. But I wanted to show them the flyers and make sure we had everything they needed for the concert. On the drive over, I felt only a slight twinge of guilt about not telling Witt. He seemed to rub some of the guys the wrong way, and I wanted to have a meeting free of friction for a change. Besides, it was Monday. He would be at work.

When I got out of the truck, the dogs trotted over to greet me. But above their cheery yapping, I heard yelling coming from the house. I paused, trying to get a sense of what the argument was about, but there were too many voices going at once. I trudged up onto the porch and banged on the door, figuring they wouldn't hear me if I knocked.

Tucker yanked open the door and glared at me. "What do you want?" he said.

Not the greeting I was hoping for, but oh well. "Is this a bad time?" I asked.

"Yeah, go away!" I couldn't see who said this, but a moment later Delilah pushed Tucker out of the way and said, "Is this business, Manager? We're in the middle of something."

"Oh. Well. I could come back another time, I guess. I just wanted to show you this." I held up a flyer.

She stood in the doorway studying it. Her expression was inscrutable. Morris could have picked up a few pointers from her. She kind of shrugged and stepped away from the door and said, "You might as well come in."

I went in and saw that they were all ranged about the living room. But what arrested my eye was the sight of Witty, front and center. I hadn't noticed his truck outside. "What are you doing here?" I asked.

"What are you doing here?" he replied, with a trace of smug mockery in his tone.

"I asked you first," I said. Childish, perhaps, but what can I say? Witt and I go back a long way.

"I have to practice," he said, again in that wisenheimer tone.

I turned to Delilah. "What's going on?"

She heaved a sort of sigh and said, "Well, Manager, it seems some people in this band didn't like the way things were going. So... Matt quit. But don't worry. We're taking on your friend here to fill in, at least until we get through the concert. After that... well, we'll see how it goes."

Witty was grinning like a dog that's found something rotten to roll in. I stared at him. "You can't play bass," I said.

"Jimmy's gonna teach him a few notes. He'll be fine," said Delilah. She tossed a smile at Witty, and he lifted his big chin like a seal catching a fish.

I could see there would be no reasoning with him. I glanced at the other guys in the band. Tucker was glowering like a silent movie villain. Jimmy's head was down, his eyes on the guitar that seemed to be welded to him. Denny was playing chords softly on his keyboard, with the resigned expression of someone who's heard it all before. Only Crater, smoking a cigarette behind his drum kit, appeared to amused by the situation. He caught my eye and winked.

I shook my head and tried to focus. "I don't understand. When did this happen? How did this happen? Can't you persuade Matt to come back? At least for the concert?"

Delilah snorted. "You have a lot to learn," she said.

"That asshole always thought he was too good for us," said Tucker.

"I'm sure that's not true," I said.

Tucker glared at me, then at Witty, and back at me. "You don't know shit. And that goes double for the meathead," he said, jerking his head in Witt's direction.

Noticing Witty's fists on red alert, I stepped up for a spot of diplomacy. "I understand that you artistic types can be sensitive to criticism, but I'm sure that Matt respects you, and anything he said was probably just a way of letting off steam. You know. He probably regrets it now."

"You don't get it," said Tucker. "That jackass got up on his high horse because Delilah and Denny got paid for that thing on Saturday, and Mr. Cool was pissed because he thought he should have been there because he thinks he's some kind of jazz expert."

Delilah put a hand on Tucker's chest and looked up into his eyes and said quietly, "Let me handle this." She turned to me and said, "Listen Manager, if you want to try to fix it, be my guest. But know this, I'm not apologizing to that jerk. He told me singers are a dime a dozen. You can tell him that any fool can play bass, and we can prove it." She glanced at Witty, who didn't seem to notice the slur.

I sighed heavily. "Where's Matt now?"

"Who cares?" said Tucker.

Delilah shook her head. "He's probably gone into D.C." She went over to the mantel and picked up a matchbook and gave it to me. "That's a place he goes to sometimes to jam. They might know where to find him."

I took the matchbook and started for the door. On the threshold, I turned back and looked at them. "If I find him, you'll take him back, right?"

No one said anything for half a minute. Delilah exchanged a glance with the boys in the band—I couldn't tell if she included Witty—then she turned to me and said, "We'll see. Let's play it by ear for now."

I took one last look at Witty. He gave me a thumbs up. The eagerness in his face was painful to behold.

I would be lying to my public if I said that my thoughts as I drove back to Dudleigh were bright and serene. Although I understand that the artistic temperament is a delicate thing, and that these creative types like to make dramatic gestures, I feel there ought to be some sort of limit, or quota. I guess, in fine, I felt somewhat betrayed. Where was the team spirit? Here I was, working my fingers to the bone, so to speak, to put on this concert for them, and this is how they repay my efforts? I found it hard to summon the will to drive all the way to D.C. on a wild goose chase to find a surly musician, who would in all likelihood spurn my efforts to bring him back to the fold.

If I weren't already so deeply in debt in this business, and if it weren't the only scheme I had for holding onto Jenny, I had half a mind to quit the whole thing. But the Moons are not quitters. Besides, I had already made plans to go into Fairfax that afternoon with Phoebe to pick up the parachutes, and the thought of this reminded me that the money-lenders Cliff had promised would be delivering the needed funds had not, as yet, done so. Then I remembered that I had given them the café as my address, and I headed there, even though it was my day off. Maybe the money was already there.

The lunch hour was winding down when I got there, and I hoped I'd be able to slip in, grab the money, and get out without getting caught up in any familial chit-chat with Glory. As it turns out, she was standing right inside the kitchen when I went in the back door.

"What brings you here, Sluggo?" she said. Her jocular tone assured me that the weekend's bumper crop of paying customers had soothed the cash flow for the nonce.

"Has there been a delivery for me here? I've been expecting something," I said.

Her expression underwent a downward shift. She grabbed hold of my sleeve and pulled me through the kitchen and into the little cupboard that serves as her office. She shut the door and turned on me. "What have you been up to now?" she hissed.

"Nothing. Pure as the driven," I protested.

"Cut the crap, Duggie. Two men came here last night after I sent you home." She gave me another look. "They were looking for you."

"Ah."

"They looked like extras from a mafia movie."

"Oh."

"Would you care to explain?"

"Um."

"I mean it, Duggie. I've given you the benefit of the doubt for years, but so help me, if you've gotten yourself in some criminal gang, I'll turn you in myself."

I shook my head vigorously. "It's not like that. I just needed to borrow some money for this concert I'm putting on. Just a short term loan. I'll be paying it back after the concert and that's that."

She shook her head slowly, looking at me with the usual expression of weary irritation. "Do you have any idea who these people are?"

"What do you mean?"

"I mean, one of them had a Russian accent. And scars on his face. They scared me. Me! And I don't scare easy, Duggie."

"Yes. I know. Listen, I'm sorry they came here. I wasn't thinking when I gave them this address. I guess I just thought it would be easier than trying to tell them how to get to my place, and I'm not always—"

"I don't care what you thought! You never think! These men looked like gangsters. I'm worried about you."

I nodded, trying to reassure her. "Listen, it's going to be all right. The concert is in less than two weeks, and then all of this will be over."

She pressed her lips together and stared at me for half a minute. "I hope you're right," she said.

I sensed that she had finished with the haranguing portion of the interview, so I said, "Did they leave the money with you?"

"What? No! They seemed a little irritated that this wasn't your home, and they asked me where you lived, and I said I couldn't tell them, and they didn't like that at all, but they said they'd find you, and if they didn't they'd be back here."

"I'm sorry, Glor. I'll make it right. I promise."

She just shook her head and gave me a pitying look. "You idiot. You shouldn't be allowed loose."

"It'll be fine. I'll take care of it."

A gentler light came into her eyes then, and she reached out and put a hand on my shoulder. "Be careful, okay?"

I assured her that I would, and left feeling as if I had just stepped out of a cold shower. I jogged to my truck and jumped in, started the engine, and put it in gear. Something banged on the door. I looked out and saw Phoebe with her hands on her hips, like a cheerleader waiting for her cue. "Hey, I thought we were going to Fairfax," she said.

Right. Right. I knew that. "Get in," I said. "We just have to make a quick stop in Springfield on the way."

CHAPTER FIFTEEN

A fronte praecipitium a tergo lupi
A precipice in front, wolves behind

She's nothing like Jenny, and it goes without saying that she could never fill the hole in my heart, but I'll say this for Phoebe, she's like a human pep pill. I don't think she took more than one or two breaths on the entire drive into Springfield. It was non-stop free-roaming enthusiasm. Starting with the band, and moving through the gig, the season, her costume plans, the personalities of various kittens and puppies currently up for adoption at the shelter, and continuing without pause into an enthusiastic response to her first sight of The Cliff at Rock Hard, she bubbled, squeaked and bounced in her seat as she chattered on and on about how super and awesome everything was.

Oddly enough, all of this undiluted positivity had the effect of making me feel somehow more—how shall I say—manly, I guess is one word for it. Being backed into the corner and forced to take on the silent, serious role in the sketch, left me feeling that I might just pull this whole concert thing off.

I got out of the truck and turned to tell Phoebe I'd be right back, but she was already skipping to the door of the gym, like a puppy bounding for the dog park. I should have known it would be her kind of place.

There was a different receptionist staring vacantly at the computer screen at the front desk, but she wore the same sort of form-fitting Lycra/spandex outfit, and directed me to Cliff's office with the same bored expression. Phoebe had vanished somewhere inside the place already.

I hurried past an array of medieval torture machines, where sweating men and glistening women were working on their abs and glutes and pecs and whatnot. The door to Cliff's personal space was ajar. I pushed it open and saw that he was bench pressing what looked to be a couple of small refrigerators. Seeing me out of the corner of his eye, he grunted, "Just one more, bro."

When the weights dropped back to the bar, he sat up and wiped his face with a towel and said, "You got your workout gear?"

"What?"

"Shorts, shoes. You're not going to work out in that are you?"

I cleared my throat. "Actually, Cliff, I didn't come to work out. Not that it wouldn't be good, too, sometime, but today I kind of need to get that money so I can pay for some supplies we need for the concert."

He stood up and came closer and gave me a penetrating once over. Then he shook his head and said, "You don't look good. You look like a man who's been neglecting his body, and it's affecting your spirit. There's like... a negative cloud around you, man. You need to dispel that if you want to be successful."

I frowned. He didn't seem to be picking up on the serious, manly side of me. "I hear what you're saying, Cliff, and I'm sure a few workouts would be great, but right now—"

He punched me on the shoulder. Hard. It hurt. "You don't get it, Moon," he said. "Right now is all there is. There's no do-overs in life. You've got to maximize every moment."

"That's what I'm trying to do, really. It's just that, right now I have a few problems I've got to sort out, and I really need that money to get working on them."

He shook his head slowly from side-to-side, looking at me as if I were the last man in a relay race, and I'd dropped the baton.

"I'm hearing a lot of negativity, Moon. That's not gonna get the job done. You have to learn to take that negative energy and flip it into positive. Then, the worse things seem, the better it is for you, get it? You got worry? Feed off it. Don't let it eat you up. That's the Marshall Plan." He punched me again. I sensed from the look in his eye that he was doing it to get me pumped, but frankly, I was feeling a bit pummeled.

I edged away from him, the better to dodge the next fist, and asked if he had the money for me.

He shrugged impatiently. "You'll get your money. Stop worrying about it."

"But, these men came to my sister's restaurant, and they didn't leave the money there and—"

"Hold it. Hold it," he interrupted. "Who came where?"

I told him about the men who came to Glory's. He frowned and said, "You mean the address you gave me wasn't your home address?"

"Well, no. You see where I live is kind of out of the way—"

"Moon, you got a lot to learn. When someone offers you a loan, and you disrespect them by giving them a phony address..." He shook his head and stared at a poster on the wall of some kick boxer flying through the air.

"No, but, it wasn't disrespect," I said. "Honest. I just live way out in the boonies, and I thought it'd be easier—"

He held up his hands to stop me. "All right. I'll take your word for it. You give me your real address. I'll pass that along. And you'll get your money. But no more funny stuff."

"Right. No. Of course. I promise. I'll give you directions and everything. And I'm sorry if I... I didn't mean..."

"It's all right. Just so you understand now."

"Sure, sure. I can see how you have to worry about people not paying you back—"

"Oh, I'm not worried. It's not my money."

"It's not?"

"Nah. It's coming from my backers."

"Who are they?"

"They're a consortium of businessmen." He gave me a look that seemed to suggest that I should be content with that answer, but, I have to say, it left me uneasy.

Cliff apparently interpreted my silence as acceptance, for he continued in a more affable tone, "I told them they could double their investment when the band hits big."

I sat down to absorb this. After a moment I said, "Really? How well do you know these guys?"

"Well enough. They sponsored my first instructional video. They love me."

"Ah." I couldn't help thinking that if these investors loved Cliff, they might find an easy-going guy like me a bit of a letdown. But then, I reflected, they didn't have to like me. They just had to like the band. "Do they know anything about the music business?"

"They don't need to. You're the expert. I told them you were a Zen master of cool."

"Well, thanks," I said, feeling a bit flattered, naturally. "But you know, the thing is... music—it's like beauty you know? In the eye, or the ear in this case, of the beholder."

Cliff looked blank, as if he were waiting for me to get to the point.

"I mean, what I'm trying to say is, I like the band, and I'm sure you'd like the band, but... let's just suppose, for the sake of argument, that we don't make as much money as we hoped. Do you think these investors would understand?"

"Moon, what did I tell you about being negative? You don't want to attract negative energy to this project. Concentrate on success!" He punched me again. In my confusion I'd let him drift into range.

Rubbing my arm, I said, "Yes, but—"

"No buts!" he said, trying to punch me again. An alert backward leap spared me.

"No maybes," Cliff continued, stalking me around the desk. "You got to believe in yourself, like Rocky. Look what it did for him."

"Yes. But, Identity Crisis isn't anything like Rocky."

"That's not the point! Focus, Moon! Visualize glory!"

Of course, then I had this sudden picture of my sister and how pissed off she was going to be if I failed to repay the paltry three hundred dollars she'd loaned me for the guitar. I couldn't imagine Cliff's backers would be any less irate if they expected to see a return on their considerably larger investment.

After another moment, during which Cliff hummed the theme from "Man of La Mancha," I asked where, exactly, these investors were located, hoping that perhaps they lived at some distance. Perhaps L.A. or Vancouver.

"They're right down the road. They've got a warehouse in Alexandria. They do a lot of import business. High end furniture and rugs. They're always looking for fresh ideas to expand their business. That's why I suggested your band to them."

"Ah." To say that this bit of news allayed my fears would be misleading my public. Still, there was nothing I could do about it now. As Julius Caesar once said, *Alea jacta est*. The die was cast. I was in too deep to pull out now. All I had to do was to make sure the concert was a success, and I'd be able to repay all my creditors with money to spare. I took a deep breath.

"Well that's fine then, I guess. But, you don't have the money now?"

"No. But I can loan you another couple hundred if that'll get you through until the boys deliver the rest."

"That would be really helpful."

He opened a drawer and pulled out an envelope and fished out a couple of crisp hundred dollar bills, which he handed to me. I thanked him and headed to the door.

"Say," he said, coming closer. "I was thinking of maybe coming to the shindig. I'd like to hear your band."

"Yeah. Sure. You should do that. It's gonna be a costume party. So," I shrugged. I couldn't picture Cliff in anything but gym shorts.

"No problem. Maybe I'll see you there." He punched me one last time. I didn't try evasive action. I had his money in my hand, after all.

I collected Phoebe from the treadmill where she was jogging. She beamed at Cliff as we left, and I saw him nod in an approving way. No doubt he could sense her positive energy clear across the room.

As it turned out a couple of hundred wasn't close to what it cost to get three parachutes, even though they were used and sold at a special discount by some guy Phoebe had found in the phone book. He assured us that, at two hundred dollars apiece, we were getting a real bargain, and Phoebe seemed to think so too, so I didn't put up much resistance when she offered to put half the cost on her credit card. I told her I'd pay her back as soon as my loan came through. She trusts me implicitly.

By the time I made it back to the shack, I was spent. A day at work would be restful compared to this.

I fed Rufie and scarfed a quick dinner, cobbled from discards of yesterday's brunch menu. If it weren't for the generous supply of crumbs from the café's kitchen, I'd have starved long before now. I sucked down a quick beer and rolled a skinny joint to take outside while I walked Rufie.

The moon was rising over the trees, full and bright and kind of pale yellow. I stared at it while Rufie tore through the underbrush, kicking up leaves. It was a nice night. Cool, but not cold. The air had that kind of leafy, smoky scent. I sat on the bottom step of the porch and smoked the joint, and kept smoking until I felt that window open in my head—the one that lets in all the good ideas. And then, of course, I knew just what to do to put this dump truck day behind me. I went inside and got my guitar and came back out and played the blues. I even sang a few lines. I hesitated for only like half a second, considering that Morris might hear me. But then, I figured, what the hell. He can always turn up his stereo. His loss.

Chapter Sixteen

Cave quid dicis, quando, et cui
Beware of what you say, when, and to whom.

Say what you will about a job that entails a lot of mindless drudgery, the next day, as I worked my way through a stack of pots and pans, I had a smile on my face, because I knew there was no chance of anyone sneaking up on me and punching me on the shoulder and expecting me to like it.

There's a window near the sink at the café, too, so if I come to work stoned, as I had today, it's almost peaceful back in my corner of the kitchen. I could hear the knives clanging out in the prep room. Every now and then, Eduardo would fire off a volley of Spanish instructions, and Mike, the new sous chef, would deliver a kind of sotto voce translation to Marcie, the girl who's learning the ropes. The whole kitchen was working along toward the lunch hour in its own seemingly chaotic but purposeful way, like some many-headed organism that understood the concept of teamwork.

This sort of deep insight often comes to me while I'm washing dishes. Especially if I've prepared myself, ahem, beforehand. And, as is often the case, one insight leads to another, and I found myself wondering why the band couldn't function with the same sort of cooperative many-headedness of the kitchen staff. Surely they weren't that far apart in terms of goals? They both aimed to please the multitudes. Both tasks require a certain artistry. But, most of all, it seems to me, both can only succeed if they work together. Each one. Not the band working with the kitchen staff. Though that might be interesting. Though messy, I suppose.

"Hey, Gandhi! Are you washing that pot or making love to it?"

Marcie, the new low-rung on the kitchen staff, has learned that if she takes a shot at me, I don't fire back. Not at the gentler sex. Even though in her case, this might be stretching the definition. She rides a Harley to work, and wears her biker boots in the kitchen. Plus she has a tattoo of a cobra on her cutting arm. These little things say so much about a girl.

Anyway, I rinsed the pot in question and handed it to her without a word. I wasn't going to let her rudeness sully my Zen state. If more people considered thus before they spoke, the world would be a far more peaceful place. Quieter, at least.

It's not my job to instruct. I try to lead by example. But today, I was mostly just glad to take a break from the stress of my new career. Every time I thought about the concert, I felt as if I'd swallowed a bit of undercooked rat and was waiting for the symptoms to manifest. This business with Matt... no. I can't think about that now. If I start trying to imagine how the band must sound with Witty fumbling along on the bass, I see a drunken parade in my head—tuba players crashing into snare drums, trombones tripping up the baton twirlers. Tragedy ensues.

"Hey, I know I'm not paying you much, but do you think you could at least pretend to be working? It's bad for the busboys' morale to see you lurking around like a panhandler."

I smiled at Glory. "Did you hear what you just said?" I asked.

"Yeah, yeah. Very funny. Seriously, are you all right?" She came closer and lowered her voice. "Have you heard any more from... those guys?"

I reeled ever so slightly. Another worry I was trying to keep buried. Oh well, sisterly concern is such an unusual thing from Glory that I didn't want to discourage her by dismissing it. So I sighed and said, "No. Not yet. But I went to the source, sort of, and it's taken care of. They won't be coming here again."

She frowned and shook her head. Then she gave me a kind of appraising look and said quietly, "Just for the record, how much are we talking about here? Because if it's just a few hundred maybe I can—"

I held up a hand to shush her, which, at any other time would have been a rare thrill in itself, but I couldn't revel in this case. "No. It's a bit more than that. Quite a bit more. But," I went on hurriedly, noting the alarm in her eyes, "it's okay. I've got everything lined up for the concert, and it's going to bring in all that I've borrowed plus a tidy profit, so I'll be paying you back and everyone else."

"Oh my god. You've been borrowing from other people too?"

I gave an equivocating shrug. "A few people have helped with some of the smaller expenses."

She stared at me with this look of horror for about half a minute, and I was just about to try to say something funny to lighten the mood, when she turned and walked away, shaking her head.

"Glor? Don't worry. It'll all come out in the wash." Not my best effort, but it's hard to shine when your audience is walking out on you. Oh well. I took it as a positive sign that she still cared enough about me to worry. Cliff would have been proud of me. When I'm stoned, I can focus on the positive for hours. Unless I get paranoid. But that wasn't going to happen today, because I had parachutes. I had porta-johns. I had—

"Seriously, dude. Get a clue." Marcie dropped a pile of greasy pans on the counter beside me and punched my arm. I gaped at her. More stunned than hurt. What was it about me that drew the fists of mine enemies?

By the time I finally finished my double shift, it was dark out. The moon hadn't risen yet. The woods around the shack were spooky with shadows and creaky sounds. I cracked open a beer and rolled a reefer and was just about to repair the damage to my nervous system from a long day of mindless toil, when Rufie started growling.

This hardly ever happens, he being in general a warm and caring soul like me—a friend to all—and the sound touched off a sudden shift into high paranoia, even though technically I wasn't yet high. Those of us who imbibe regularly have a kind of residual paranoia that never fully disengages. If my experience with the pot bus last summer taught me anything, it was this: They really are all out to get you. Only by ceaseless vigilance can you evade their snares.

So, with this in mind, I quietly stashed the joint under a book and went to the window. Peeking through the shade, I couldn't see much because of the darkness, but the stray light from the shack revealed a strange car parked beside the truck. At first I thought maybe Cheyenne was back for more of the Moon charisma, but the car, a vintage Thunderbird, didn't look familiar. I would have remembered if she'd been driving that. It looked pretty sweet, in fact. I was half-tempted to go outside and take a look, but the sound of feet clumping up the porch steps restored my paranoia to its previous early-warning level. I stepped back from the window and waited. Whoever was out there waited also. Maybe they'd seen me at the window and were waiting for me to open the door.

Hah. As if. Maybe they hadn't seen me at the window, and if I stayed quiet they'd just go away. But maybe it was someone I knew. Anyone who owned a car that cool couldn't be a cop, right?

I probably could have gone on considering these and other questions for some time, but whoever was out on the porch seemed to be coming to a decision. There were muttering voices, and then a bang on the door, followed by another burst of muttering and then a short civil knock, of the sort used to introduce a knock, knock joke.

My curiosity was running neck and neck with my paranoia by this time. Rufie was still growling, low and steady, like a motorboat engine in neutral, so I figured he had my back. I opened the door.

There were two men standing there, squinting into the light behind me. One was as tall as I am, with a beaky nose and hooded eyes. His blond hair was slicked back off his face, which was pale above the stubbled jawline. The shorter guy was dressed in a pinstripe suit, the kind you see in old gangster movies. He had a nose like a knobbly potato, and his face looked like a ball of dough that's been punched a few times. As soon as I saw them, I realized who they had to be. I was so glad they weren't cops that I smiled and said, "Hi. You must be Cliff's friends. Come in."

They exchanged a mute glance and stepped in. They both looked around the room as if they were thinking of renting, and they weren't too impressed.

"So, thanks for coming," I said. "I'm sorry I gave you the wrong address at first. I didn't think you'd want to come all this way."

The shorter man looked at me without smiling. After a few seconds he said, "We know now where you live." He had an accent. Something Eastern European, maybe?

"Ah well. You're not from around here, are you?" I said, trying to keep it light. "It's easy to get lost in these mountains."

He gave me another long look. Then he said, "Is easy for fire trucks to get lost."

I hesitated, trying to decide if that was meant as a joke or a threat. I decided to give him the benefit of the doubt and changed the subject. "That's a great car you have. I love those old Thunderbirds. What year is it?"

The shorter man's expression shifted, as if the dough in his face was getting warm and starting to rise. "Is a 1971." He pushed his lips up and out, like he was thinking about something. Then he reached inside his jacket, and I flinched just a bit until he pulled out a bulging envelope. He held it out to me.

"Count it."

"Oh I'm sure it's all there. I trust you."

"Count it."

I took the bills out and counted them quickly. "Yup. It's all here. Thanks so much for bringing it. Would you like a beer or anything?"

The skinny guy shot a glance at the fridge, but the guy in the suit said, "We leave now. We know where you live. We'll be back."

"Right. Of course. And I'll pay this back to you. Every penny."

"And twenty percent."

I frowned. "I'm sorry. What did you say?"

"Twenty percent. You give back the money and twenty percent."

"Wait, um. Cliff never said anything about twenty percents. Are you sure that's right?"

"I'm sure."

"But, twenty percent... that's um, six hundred, right?"

"You pay back right away, is six hundred. Twenty percent. You are late, is thirty."

"What? Wait. What do you mean by late? How late is late? What if I don't have all the money collected right away?"

"We come back in two weeks. Twenty percent. You don't have it, we come back one week later, thirty percent. You still don't pay?" He paused and shook his head. "You don't want that to happen." He looked around the shack and back at me. "Fire trucks get lost." He shrugged.

I swallowed. A cold sweat was running down my neck. Could I just give the money back now? No. It was too late. I had to go through with the concert. "Okay. I understand. I'll have the money," I said.

"Good." He noticed one of the flyers taped to the wall. "I-dent-it-y Cri-sis," he said, slowly, as if weighing the merits of the name. He turned to me. "Are they good band?"

"Oh yeah. They're great. You should hear them."

He exchanged a look with his partner. "Maybe we come to the party."

"Oh yeah. Sure. That'd be great," I lied. Just what I didn't need. A couple of rug-dealing thugs at the party.

They drove away, and I sank onto the couch and let the waves of terror wash over me, until I remembered I had a joint ready to go. I fired it up and sucked down another beer and told myself everything would be fine. Fine. Fine.

Then I got out the guitar and played the blues. After a while I started to feel more calm. After all, I told myself, there was no point in worrying about what might happen. For the moment, all was well. I had a plan. I had my guitar. I had Rufie. And sure, maybe I had the blues right now. But like the man said, the blues ain't nothin' but a good woman on your mind. I don't know who this man was. But I can only assume he spoke from experience. The Romans don't have much to say on the subject. Presumably conquering the known world was an effective means of avoiding the blues.

CHAPTER SEVENTEEN

Vitam regit fortuna, non sapienta
Fortune, not wisdom, rules lives.
Cicero

You know how they say you can fool all of the people some of the time and some of the people all of the time, but you can't fool all of the people all of the time? Well, fooling people has never been my strong suit, but I do believe that in order to live in this world, it helps to be able to fool yourself a certain amount of the time, because otherwise, if you really think about it, life is kind of a one-way highway to oblivion, and who wants to dwell on that? I mean, *tempus edax rerum* and all that, and of course that's true, but even so, you have to keep getting through the day. The trick is to sweep all that grim stuff under the rug of the unconscious and leave it there. However, as anyone who's tried this knows, the stuff under the carpet comes creeping out while you're asleep.

Suffice it to say, I wasn't feeling rested as I worked my way through the lunch hour dishes. But I'd eased Glory's mind when I paid her back, so I hoped she'd be willing to let me off early tonight. I need some time to address the list of things I have to get done before the concert. I mean, on the one hand, you think to yourself, how hard can it be? But on the other hand, it's like learning to juggle. You start off with two oranges, and it's a snap. Then you add an apple, and it gets a little tricky. Then you keep adding, a couple of eggs, a melon, a chainsaw...

All this added tension was putting a strain on my stash, too, and, since I've been trying to maintain a cleanish slate at the shack, in case Sheriff Quayle decides to make a surprise inspection, I don't have the kind of reserve that I once did. I really needed to make a another visit to Darren, and planned to slip out between the lunch and dinner shifts today.

I was jogging out to the truck, when my cell phone rang. I considered letting it ring. So far, my experience with this high tech ball and chain has shown that it's almost never a source of glad tidings. However, on the chance that it could be Jenny with a change of heart, I flipped it open. A female voice started in a mile a minute, the way they sometimes do.

"Manager, we have a problem."

I bowed the head briefly, bracing for the next blow.

"What's up?"

"Your buddy Whitmore? He's not really picking up the bass as quick as I'd hoped."

I rolled the eyes. Not that she could see this, but it gave some relief for the irritation. Of course a sausage-fingered blockhead like Witty couldn't be expected to pick up an instrument, even one with only four strings, and play it as if he had rhythm in his bones. He has no shortage of romance in his soul, but digital dexterity, not so much.

I sighed. "I'm sorry to hear that. What do you want me to do about it?"

"I want you to go find that whiner and bring him back."

"And by 'whiner' you mean—"

"You know who I mean. That prima donna who thinks he's too good for the rest of us. As far as I'm concerned he can rot in hell, but we need him for this concert, and he owes us that much. After it's over he can vanish for all I care, but you've got to make him come back and play for this if you don't want us to stink the joint out."

"It's that bad, huh?"

"It's worse than that. And he annoys the crap out of the guys. He's nice enough around me, but we know why that is. The guys can't use him at all. The sooner you get Matt back here, the better."

"Have you heard from him?"

"No. He'd never call. He's too full of himself. You might have to beg to get him to come back. But that's part of your job."

"Right. Okay. I'm on it."

I shut the phone and tried to think how I could get time off to go into D.C. on a wild goose chase. I couldn't afford to waste a minute, which meant putting off replenishing my stash. I started trudging back to the café, trying to think how to persuade Glory to let me have another day off. She wasn't going to like it. The Leafers were still swarming.

I was sitting on the steps outside the back door, working on my argument, when the cell phone rang again. I opened it quickly, hoping maybe Delilah had heard from Matt, and I was off the hook.

"Moon. How's it going?" Cheyenne's take-charge tone came through all too loud and clear.

I considered for a moment whether I could snap the phone shut and pretend it had dropped the call. But if she called right back, it would only be more awkward. So I steeled the nerves and said, "Hi. It's going well. How are you?"

She laughed. A short bemused kind of 'hah.' I didn't know what that meant, so I maintained a cautious silence.

After a few seconds she said, "I thought I might hear from you by now. You know? With some feedback on the flyers. I've seen them around town."

"Oh, yeah. They're great. Everybody likes them."

"Hmm. Well, the reason I'm calling is, your gig is a week from Saturday, right?"

"Right."

"So, the thing is, a lot of times when you're banking on flyers for your publicity, it's a good idea to refly a few days before the event."

"Refly?"

"Yeah. You know. Splash another round out there. Not exactly the same, but using some of the same colors to tie in to the first round. On Halloween weekend there's a lot going on. You don't want your old flyers to get papered over by some other monster mash. A refly keeps the buzz building. You've got to make your gig the one no one wants to miss."

I frowned. I could see where this was going.

"How much would that cost?"

"For you, I could whip it out and get you five hundred by early next week for, let's say, two hundred."

I knew it. Luckily, any starry-eyed dreams I'd had of actually making any money from this enterprise were long gone, so I didn't hesitate.

"Sure. That sounds like a good thing to do, I guess."

There was a moment of silence on her end. I thought for a minute perhaps she'd already hung up, and I would have accepted that without a murmur, but then she piped up again. "You don't sound too upbeat, Moon. What's the matter? Are you out of pot?"

I sat up a bit, startled by her acuity. "It's not that."

"What's the problem?"

I sighed again. I didn't know whether to give her the whole story, complete with footnotes on Witty's romantic delusions, but I began explaining, and it all sort of spilled out. "So, that's the situation. I don't know if I can do it," I concluded.

There was like half a second of delay, and then the bomb went off. "Well, snap out of it, Moon! If you want to be a manager, you have to manage! That means take charge! You got a rogue bass player, you don't just let him wander off into traffic—especially if your only alternative is some doofus who can't play a lick. Go after

146

him! Which one left? The one who looks like Keith Richards before heroin?"

"I can't picture that."

"He's the one who looks like the angel of doom, right? All in black."

"They all wear black. Except for Tucker. But he usually takes his shirt off so maybe—"

"Moon. Moon. Focus. I don't need a fashion report. Tell you what. You're obviously stressed out about this, and rightfully so. I'll back you up. I'll come with you. I can drive, save you gas money. You find out where he is. We'll go get him tonight."

"Tonight?"

"There's no time to lose. You've got a bad situation. You don't want to let it fester. What if somebody else quits? You've got to keep that band together, whatever it takes. At least until after Halloween."

I considered this. She was right. And, much as I didn't particularly want to surrender control to this female dynamo, there was no question that having her at my side would likely improve my chances of bringing Matt back. I had a momentary vision of Cheyenne pinning his arm behind his back and forcing him into the car. Such strong arm tactics would be beyond my scope, but she could do it. She'd probably enjoy it.

"Okay. Thanks."

We agreed that she would pick me up at the café when she got off work. With any luck we'd be in D.C. before seven.

Of course, I hadn't told her that all I had to go on in the way of finding Matt was a matchbook. Maybe that would be enough. Bloodhounds succeed with less.

By ten o'clock, I was thinking wistfully about bloodhounds while Cheyenne was shooting the breeze with the bartender at The Lucky Loser, the run-down club where the bartender at the last place we'd checked had said he thought Matt might be playing tonight. The first place, the matchbook place, The Lowdown, turned out to be a hole in the wall about the size of my shack that had a jukebox crammed with jazz classics. A saxophone player and a drummer were doodling in the corner when we got there at around eight. The bartender had no idea who we were talking about, until Cheyenne brought up the Keith Richards motif, and then he said he might have seen someone like that the night before last. Big help.

Cheyenne got him to give her a list of places where jazz players could sit in, and we were off. It reminded me a little of being on a scavenger hunt. Except we didn't need to collect a bunch of little items. Just one big one.

At least Cheyenne was enjoying herself. She seemed right at home schmoozing with the bartenders. She kept offering me drinks, but I wanted to stay sharp. I didn't know what kind of mood Matt would be in, if and when we found him, but I wanted to be ready if he decided to work off some of his frustration on me. I'd had enough of being punched. I planned to run like the wind.

"Nathan thinks Matt might show up here in the next hour." Cheyenne slid next to me in the booth where I was nursing a ginger ale. Her thigh pressed against mine in a manner that I can only describe as aggressively suggestive, and I was already as far away on the bench seat as I could get. The only escape left would be to slide under the table and slither out the other side. I hoped it wouldn't come to that.

"What makes him think Matt's going to show up?" I asked.

"He says there's a piano player who usually stops in around eleven and plays a few songs. He says Matt's jammed with the guy a few times. So..." she shrugged. "It's worth a shot."

I shrugged in agreement. Although, in my heart of hearts, I had already come to think this whole venture was an insane waste of time and energy. In the last hour I'd had a brilliant idea, which I wasn't about to share with Cheyenne, for fear it would lead to a frenzy of shoulder punching and high fiving, she being of the Cliff Marshall school of team building. But, just between ourselves, it had occurred to me that while Witty hadn't been able to master the rudiments of bass playing in a few days, I, having already logged in a certain amount of basic training on my trusty guitar, might be able to make the transition to bass with more ease. Okay. Maybe ease is not the right word. But I bet I could fake my way through a few songs better than Witt. So I was feeling ever so slightly better, with this fallback plan in mind.

There was a guitarist diddling from one song to another up near the door. I didn't recognize anything, although every now and then he'd play one line that sounded familiar, but it never amounted to a whole song. You know, the kind with verses and choruses and whatnot. I think that's really what I have against jazz. It's not that I don't respect it and all. But sometimes I think jazz players just go out of their way to make it confusing. Maybe it's an acquired taste.

Cheyenne was staring at the door the whole time, like a cat zoned in on a mouse hole. From time to time she patted my thigh with her left hand under the table, in what, I imagine, she considered a reassuring manner. To say it made me feel better would be misleading my public.

I was just about to make a break for the open air, when she squeezed my thigh a lot harder and said in a husky whisper, "There's our boy."

I followed her gaze and saw a tall, dark figure carrying a bass case, slouching past the small stage. The guitar player nodded at him, and as he passed under the dim stage light, I saw that it was indeed Matt. I took a deep breath. Now came the tricky part.

We had discussed how to handle this on the way in, and we had agreed that it would be best to lay low and let him play a set first before we approached him. The idea was, we would ply him with flattery first, then switch to pleading, progressing to bribery if needed. Only if all these methods failed, would we switch to coercion. Cheyenne favored an intermediate stage of seduction, but I vetoed that idea as too chancy. Matt was no starry-eyed sucker like Witty. He could have his pick of ripe young things if he wanted them. I didn't want to offend Cheyenne, but she had to be in her mid-twenties at least, and a woman with her brusque manner is something of a specialized taste. Like jazz, I suppose you could say. It's possible that Matt might be intrigued. But we didn't have time to gamble on risky strategies.

Cheyenne had agreed to my reasoning in the car on the way in, but I could tell she wasn't feeling bound by mere words at the moment. She had let go of my thigh, and she was staring at Matt as if he were the hot new stallion in the stable, and she had a brand new riding crop.

If I'd been worried that he would spot us in the room and get defensive, I needn't have bothered. He never took his eyes off his bass, except to exchange a mumbled word or two with the guitar player. Within a few minutes, they launched into another song I didn't recognize, but I'll say this, it sounded a lot better with Matt bringing the muscle. In Identity Crisis you really don't hear the bass all that clearly, it being buried under all the lead guitar riffs and the singing and the drums smashing away. But here in this almost empty little club, the bass carried you along like the tide, coming at you in powerful waves that lifted you off your feet sometimes but always kept you moving. I have to say, I was impressed. I never knew he could play like this.

I glanced over at Cheyenne, and whoa. She had that look in her eye. And relieved as I was that she was no longer directing it at me, I couldn't help wondering if it might make things more, how shall we say, sticky, when it came time to reel in the wandering bass player.

Still, I reflected as they began another song, at least we had him in our sights. And, one thing you have to say for Cheyenne: she gave the distinct impression of being a woman who gets what she wants. And there was no doubt whatsoever what she wanted at this moment.

When the duo put down their instruments and started toward the bar, Cheyenne was out of her seat and closing in on Matt before I said a word. He never saw her coming. I decided it might be better if I let her get a head start. After all, he had never seemed particularly swayed by the Moon charm. After a couple of minutes of her doing most of the talking and him taking her in with those deep set eyes of his, he shot a glance in my direction. His expression soured at the sight of me, but then she leaned closer and whispered something in his ear, and a flicker of amusement flashed across his face before he turned back to her. I watched as they ordered drinks and sat at the bar. I decided it might be best to leave it all in her hands, one of which at the moment was caressing the back of his neck. He didn't seem to be resisting.

When he went back up to the stage, Cheyenne returned to the booth and said quietly, "Everything's under control. He's going to do the concert."

"That's great! What did you say to him?"

"I just told him I was really looking forward to seeing him on Halloween."

"That's it? That's all you said? How do you know—"

"Duggie." She lowered her chin and looked at me seriously and said, "He's going to do the concert. No promises after that. But you can take it from me: he's playing with the band for the concert."

"And afterwards?"

"He'll be playing with me."

CHAPTER EIGHTEEN

Spectaculorum procedere debet
The show must go on.

Aside from making a quick call to Delilah to tell her that Matt was back on board, I tried to put the whole thing out of my mind for the next couple of days. It wasn't easy. Every time I closed my eyes, visions of Cheyenne, rubbing up against Matt like a cat that wanted to be picked up, flickered across my retina. Not that I have anything against cats, or Cheyenne, but, you know how it is. In general one would prefer not to witness the mating rituals of casual acquaintances.

Fortunately, Glory was in high gear when I got to work the next day, and there were no opportunities for quiet reflection. The atmosphere in the kitchen reminded me of those scenes in Star Trek when the Klingons are throwing everything in their arsenal at the good ship, and the crew somehow manage to keep all systems going, while darting for cover and dodging shrapnel. It's not exactly restful, but it's diverting.

By the time the last dinner guest stumbled out to the parking lot, I wanted only to find a quiet spot to lie down, possibly after smoking a nice fat joint, if I could eke one out of my dwindling stash. On the quiet drive back to the shack, I considered whether it might be worth the aggravation to stop over at Morris's first, in the hope that he might relent and share some of his secret reserve. He thinks I don't know about it, and, I can't say I have any hard proof, but the fact is, when he saved my neck last summer by arranging for the pot bus to drive into the sunset before the sheriff's men got there, I'm reasonably certain that he set aside a few choice buds for himself. It's what I would have done, and Morris is a bit of a connoisseur. Those plants were going to be awesome.

But when I got to the turn to his house, I had second thoughts. I was too tired to put up with the requisite banter, so I went home. I shut off the engine, and immediately the sound of Rufie slobbering happily on the door reminded me that there are more important things than getting stoned.

"Hey buddy. Sorry I'm so late. You hungry?" I got out and gave him a hug and started for the porch with him leaping happily beside me. When I got there, Orson jumped down from his perch and rubbed against my leg in a rare display of what passes for affection in the feline cosmos, so, all in all, I felt I'd made the right decision.

After I fed them both, and Rufie and I played outside in the moonlight for a while, I went in. I scraped together enough for one puny joint and was starting to feel almost at peace, when I heard a truck drive up. It was loud, and backfired like a cherry bomb when the engine stopped, which told me that it could only be one person.

A few seconds later he banged once on the door and came in.

He glowered at me and said, "You happy now?"

I guessed he must have heard from Delilah that his services as a bass player were no longer required, but I decided to play it cool. It was possible he didn't know the full extent of my betrayal.

"Shouldn't I be?"

He stared at me darkly, probably searching for something clever to say, but Witt's never at his best in the cut and thrust of debate, and when his emotions are aroused, he's more inclined to say it with fists. These were curled at his side at the moment, and although I'm sure he would have been happy to apply them to some of the band members, he knew that wouldn't get him anywhere with Delilah.

"You heard what happened?"

"I talked to Delilah. She told me Matt's back in the band," I said.

Witty snorted and kicked the end of the couch. Then he sat down and said, "They never wanted me in the band. If Delilah hadn't stuck up for me..." He frowned, then looked at me and noticed the state of my stash. "That's all you got? Shit, Duggie. I knew you wouldn't be any help, but I thought I could at least get a buzz on if I came here."

I sighed. "I didn't have time to get over to see Darren. I've been pulling double shifts so I can get time off next weekend for the concert."

He nodded and accepted the skinny reefer I'd cobbled together. After a couple of deep tokes he said, "So you can't play cards tomorrow?"

"Is Randall hosting?"

"Yup."

"Is he counting on me to bring the refreshments?"

"Y'always do."

"Yeah. Well. I don't even know if I'll be able to get over there. I'm working the dinner shift, and it won't be over till after ten. I'm fried."

Witty nodded, his angry fire reduced to glowing embers. "Yeah, well." He exhaled a long plume of smoke and said, "She wants me to be her bodyguard."

"Really? That's a great idea."

"I guess so. I just hope one of those twerps gets up in her face."

"What twerps?"

"Any one of 'em. That asshole drummer. That thinks-he's-so-cool bass player." He was pounding a meaty fist against his other hand. His eyes had a faraway look of righteous wrath.

I cleared my throat. "Um, yes, well. I hope it won't come to that. At least not until the concert's over."

He sniffed derisively. "It's not all about you, you know."

"I understand that. I'm just, you know, thinking about what's best for everyone. Including Delilah."

The light in his eyes dimmed. "Right. I gotta be cool. She's counting on me."

"That's right. So... we'll both do whatever it takes, right?"

"Right." He got up and paced over to the refrigerator, opened it, and said, "Man, you don't even have any beer? What's wrong with you?"

"It's a cash flow thing."

"You're pathetic."

I let this go. I could have argued the point, but, quite honestly, I was suddenly overcome by the urgent desire for sleep, and I was hoping he'd go away quietly.

In the event, he must have, because next thing I knew I was waking up on the couch, still in my work clothes. I sat up groggily and glanced at the clock. It was nine-ish. I didn't have to be at work for an hour. I lay back down and tried to fall back asleep, but you know how it is. The brain starts turning over like an engine, and the fumes of thought destroy all peace. What was it the fellow said? "Speculation is the enemy of calm." Something like that.

In the end I settled for a leisurely breakfast at the café. But as I was starting on my second cup of coffee, a shadow fell across the table and, looking up, I saw Babe McLaren. She sat down across from me and rested her large well-muscled arms on the table. I couldn't help feeling a bit dwarfed. Although she's an all-around athlete, her legend was founded on a landmark arm-wrestling victory over Marlowe Smoot. I hadn't seen much of her since the softball tournament, but I assumed she'd been busy with her landscaping business.

She was giving me the sad eye, as if she knew of my secret sorrow, and I suddenly realized that, of course, it would be hers too.

"How're you holdin' up, Duggie?" she asked.

I shrugged. "I'm okay."

She nodded and kind of stuck her chin up. "We got to let her go."

"I know."

She shook her head. "I just wish she wasn't going with that creep."

Music to my ears. "I know."

"That guy's got liar written all over him, but she doesn't see it."

"I know. But what can we do?"

She shook her head. "I know what I'd like to do," she said darkly, pounding her right fist into her left hand, a natural movement for a catcher.

Then a softer look came into her eye, and she said, "I know what you must be going through. We just gotta have faith that she'll come back to us."

I nodded. "I'm hoping a miracle will happen, and she won't go."

Babe shook her head. "Nah. She wants to go. We got to respect that. She deserves all the best. You know?"

"Yeah, I know."

She shifted her weight and pushed against the table to stand up. "Well, I just wanted to tell you I understand what you're going through. And if you want someone to talk to, well, I don't really want to talk. But we could hang out, have a beer maybe. Compare notes. If you hear from her, or I do."

"Right. I appreciate that."

She started toward the door, but she stopped halfway and turned her head. "Marilyn told me you're puttin' on some Halloween party at the Hangar. That right?"

"Yeah. You should come. It's a good band. I think Jenny's coming."

"Hmm. Maybe. See you."

I hadn't given any thought to how Jenny's leaving would affect anyone else. Obviously Babe was feeling it. They had been teammates for so many years, all through high school, and since Jenny moved out to Rapidan County, they just took up right where they left off. Jenny pitching, Babe catching.

I sat at the table for a few minutes, lost in thought. They were the kind of thoughts I'd been trying to ignore ever since Jenny told me she was really going. Maybe it's because Babe is usually so tough. But she was hurting now. And I knew just how she felt.

I stood up and headed back to the kitchen, ready for another marathon at the sinks. The day passed in a blur of steam and smoke. I may have sat down for five minutes somewhere around four o'clock, but it wasn't near enough.

Saturday was déjà vu all over again. The parking lot was crammed with cars with D.C. tags. You'd think they didn't have trees in the city. And it's not as if the trees on the Blue Ridge turn those kind of psychedelic shades of orange and red that give New England autumns something to brag about. No. Our Virginia palette is more muted, like something selected by a really expensive designer, in shades with names like taupe and butterscotch and persimmon. Still, it's mesmerizing in its own way. And it's a big boost for the local apple growers and trinket sellers. But from the vantage point of the kitchen sink at the Moonlight Café, you don't see many trees. By the time I slunk out of there late that night, there was a chilly wind blowing, and leaves were skittering across the empty parking lot. All I wanted to do was sleep for about forty-eight hours.

The next day a miracle occurred. Before I opened my eyes, I heard the sound, and it had been so long since I'd heard it that at first I thought I was still dreaming. But then there was an accompanying rumble of sheet metal thunder, and I sat up and looked out at the rain streaming down the window. Hallelujah! There was no way the

Leafers would be back today. Maybe I could come home after the brunch shift.

As I'd suspected, the rain scared off most of the customers. Even the brunch crowd was scanty. Glory took one look at my face and told me to leave at noon. She didn't have to tell me twice.

When I got back to the shack I was feeling so relieved that I sat down and made a list of all the things I still needed to do for the concert, and it was a lot shorter than it had been a week earlier. All that remained was to line up the keg delivery, find someone to take charge of selling beer at the concert, and make sure the porta-johns got installed before Saturday. Also, I had to help Phoebe get the parachutes up, and get a cash box and few other things, but, all in all, I was set. Except for my costume. After some thought, I'd decided to rent a full tux, with tails. I figure if I'm to have any chance of dazzling Jenny, I have to pull out all the stops.

I was sitting back, strumming a few chords on my guitar, feeling relatively at ease, when a car pulled up outside. I took a quick peek and was ecstatic to recognize Jenny's car. What a day this was turning into! My elation was short-lived, as I saw that it was Eric and Amanda who scrambled out into the rain and came squishing through the puddles to the door. They knocked lightly, and I tried to mask my disappointment.

"Hey Duggie. We went by the café, but Glory said she'd sent you home, so we thought, what the heck. Are we interrupting anything?" Eric was eyeing me like a doctor checking for signs of relapse in a patient who's just passed the critical stage.

"No. You're fine. Come on in," I said.

They sat together on the couch, close, as if they were stitched together. I couldn't help feeling envious. But nobody deserves to be happy more than Eric, and Amanda being Jenny's sister, of course I want her to be happy too. So. Anyway. I looked at them expectantly, waiting for them to cough up the real reason they came by. Because, let's face it, most of the time these lovebirds just wanted to get off by themselves and do that thing lovebirds do. If they were here on a rainy Sunday, it wasn't for entertainment purposes.

"I notice you're driving Jenny's car," I said, trying to get the ball rolling.

Amanda kind of squinched up her face, as if she'd bit into a lemon. She stole a quick glance at Eric and said, "That's kind of why we're here."

"Oh?"

Eric patted Amanda's thigh and gave her a little nod, as couples do when they tag-team a conversation. Eric seemed to want the baton, and Amanda appeared relieved. "It's like this, Duggie. Well, first of all, the reason we've got Jenny's car is that she gave the keys to Amanda, because she won't need the car while she's in France, and Amanda's car has been acting kind of flakey lately, so..."

"So I get to use Jenny's car as long as she's gone," Amanda finished quickly. I got the feeling the automotive theme was just the prelude to whatever had brought them here. It's not like my shack is on the way to anywhere else.

"The thing is," Eric continued, taking the reins again, "we're a little worried about Jenny."

Amanda nodded vigorously. I sagged in my seat. A dull dread began creeping in the pit of my stomach.

"Why?" I said.

"Well, it's kind of hard to describe, but, you know Jenny, so you know how she normally is. She doesn't let other people push her around," Amanda said.

I was baffled. What were they getting at?

"The thing is," Eric began again, "we think Jenny's not herself around this guy."

"What do you mean?"

"I mean, she's letting him call all the shots. Like, the car, for instance. It was his idea for her to give it to Amanda."

"But that seems kind of practical doesn't it?"

"Maybe. But he insisted that Jenny had to do it right away. He claims that it's too much of a hassle to find a parking space in Georgetown, and so now Jenny has no car of her own."

I frowned, considering this. "I guess that's kind of a pain."

"Yeah. It means if Jenny wants to go anywhere, she has to ask him to drive her. He doesn't let her drive his BMW."

"That doesn't seem right."

"Exactly! That's what I said," Amanda piped up. "But when I asked her about it, she just kind of shrugged it off and said it wasn't important, that Miles knows best. Just between us, I'm not so sure he's thinking of what's best for her. She's under his thumb, and I don't like it."

I tried to picture this—Jenny taking orders from Brandon. I couldn't believe she'd do it. But Amanda and Eric were clearly upset. They drove all the way out here in the rain.

"What can I do about it?" I asked, feeling helpless and bitter. I'd tried to be understanding of Jenny's desire to see the world and expand her horizons and all, but if this guy is making her forget who she really is, what can I do?

"I don't know, Duggie. Maybe there's nothing anyone can do. But we know you really love Jenny, and we thought you should know that... I'm just worried about my sister." A tear trickled down Amanda's cheek as she said this, and Eric put his arm around her and applied the comforting squeeze.

They left pretty soon after that. I tried to shrug off the feeling of gloom they'd left behind. Maybe they were just overreacting, the way these passionate lovers do. Yet as I stared out at the sodden brown leaves covering the grass, it was hard to dismiss what they'd said. Jenny had dated others guys before, during the long years of our friendship, before it became more than that. None of those guys worried me much, because even when she was with them, I could catch her eye and see the girl I loved, and I could tell she wasn't serious about anyone else. But this situation with Brandon sounded sinister.

I tried to improve my mood by playing some guitar, but even the blues were no help. With all this weighing on me, the long afternoon off wasn't the restorative I'd hoped it would be. I could have gone out and tried to distract myself at the Toad, I suppose, but my heart wasn't in it.

When it began to get dark around six, I was contemplating slogging through the rain up to Morris's. Even his sharpest barbs would be preferable to this dull misery. Then, just when I was thinking the day couldn't get worse—you guessed it.

The phone rang. I didn't recognize the number on the little screen, but I answered anyway, because I had nothing better to do, and immediately my hope rocketed back into fighting form.

"Duggie?"

"Hi. It's good to hear your voice," I said, upbeat as all get out.

I detected a fraction of hesitation on her end. I plunged into the vacuum. "Things are going great with the concert. The band is really psyched, and Phoebe's doing decorations and—"

"Duggie?" She interrupted. I swallowed and tried to shake off a dark premonition.

"That's really why I'm calling." She hesitated again, but I couldn't summon The Force to throw more positive energy at her. I didn't want to make it harder for her.

"I want you to know, I really wanted to go, but Miles just found out that he has to go to some kind of artists' reception here in town, and he can't get out of it. There will be a lot of important people there, he says. And you know, he really wanted to come hear your band again, so he's disappointed too. But, since we're leaving for Paris on Sunday, he says maybe it's for the best. I'm not even going to the reception with him, because we've got a lot of packing and things to take care of still. So... I'm really sorry."

This time I hesitated, as it sank in that she was saying goodbye... that I wasn't even going to see her again before she left... that everything I'd been working on was...

"Duggie? Are you okay? You know if there was any way I could come to the concert, I would. Just to see you."

I closed my eyes and took a deep breath. I pictured her on the other end of the line, and... that didn't make this any better. I opened my eyes and said, "I understand. I'm sorry you can't come. I could come in and get you and bring you back afterward."

"That's really sweet, but I think... maybe it's best if I just do the work Miles wants me to do. I'll call you once we're settled over there, and you can tell me all about the concert."

I wanted to throw the damned phone across the room, but I held on and said, "You know you can call me anytime. You don't have to wait till you're settled. Maybe you won't like it over there."

She didn't say anything right away. Then she said in a kind of quick broken sort of way, like she didn't want to hurt me, "I'll be back in the spring."

That did it. I couldn't speak.

"Goodbye, Duggie. I love you."

"Bye," I croaked. She knows damn well I love her.

How long I sat there after she hung up, I couldn't tell you. I might have been sitting there still, had it not been for Rufie, my faithful sidekick, whose wet nose and insistent paw finally broke through my torpor and reminded me that in spite of everything, life goes on, dogs must be walked, debts must be paid, etc. Jenny or no Jenny, I had to go forward with the concert. But I sure as hell wasn't going to try to get through the coming week straight.

I threw on a coat and boots and headed out into the night with Rufie. I didn't have to tell him where we were headed. He bounded up the path to Morris's.

My earlier reservations about Morris's superior attitude had vanished about the time Jenny announced she wouldn't be coming to the concert. Morris's habitual condescension was nothing to me now. He could ridicule me all he liked, as long as he got me stoned.

When he opened the door, he took one long look at me, no doubt registering the rain dripping freely from head to toe and the unmasked woe on my face. He gestured for us to come in. Rufie declined, preferring the bracing, night air on the porch.

Inside, Morris didn't say a word until after he'd rolled a jumbo doobie, lit it, and passed it to me. He waited another couple of minutes, and then he said, "I take it some new crisis has occurred?"

I nodded and took another hit. After I exhaled and coughed a bit, I said, "Jenny can't come to the concert."

"Ah. Unfortunate."

"So everything I've been working on for the last month is for nothing."

He shrugged. "No good effort is wasted."

I chuckled. "I am no good effort."

Morris leaned back in his chair and observed me with a kind of paternal glint in his eye. "That's the spirit," he said.

I sighed. "It probably wouldn't have worked anyway."

"The plan to win back your lady love?"

"Right."

"Perhaps not."

"And now I'll never know."

"Perhaps not."

I shot a glance up at him from where I was sitting on the floor. His head was wreathed in smoke, and his eyes were half-shut the way they get when he starts tuning in to the mystic wisdom-of-the-Orient channel.

"Don't tell me all of this is going to make me a better man," I said.

He gave me a little smile. "I wouldn't dream of it."

"I'm as good as I'm going to be."

"Perhaps."

I frowned. Fine. What do I care if he wants to float off on his cloud of vague fortune cookie prognostication? He doesn't know it all. Granted, he knows more than I do. But so what? It was his idea for me to manage a band in the first place. Hah! I could throw that in his face, but, not now, while I'm pleasantly baked from his stash. Even if it's really my stash. I don't care whose it is right now. I'm just going to lie back and close my eyes and think happy thoughts. Jenny will come back to me. How could she not? We're meant for each other. Everyone knows. It's destiny. I just have to be patient.

I may have lost track of things there for a while, because the next thing I remember is being back out in the rain, only this time I was heading home, and Rufie was trotting beside me to keep me on the path, which was pretty dark and slippery. I may have fallen down once or twice, which would explain the state of my pants. Anyway. By the time I collapsed on my own bed, I was still down, but not out. At least not for a few minutes.

CHAPTER NINETEEN

Ne cede malis, sed contra audentior
Do not yield to misfortunes, but go forth more boldly to meet them.
Virgil

The next day I wasn't as hung-over as I would have been, had I spent the evening with Witty, crying in his beer at the Toad, not that he ever cries, but you know what I mean. Whining at the very least. Yet in spite of the fact that I had gotten royally peened the night before, I felt full of high-test and ready to roll.

Which was good, because this was my last day off before the concert, and I had a zillion details to nail down. After a quick jog with Rufie, I climbed into the truck and set out to conquer the world, or at least as much of it as I could get to in the next eight or nine hours. I headed straight to Charlottesville first, to check in with Cheyenne and arrange for the refly operation. If my loyal public is surprised to learn that I was seeking out this bossy female of my own free will, they may take it as evidence of how armed and confident I felt. Also, I was fairly certain that her new fixation on the churlish bass player would keep her attention from wandering back to me.

And it turned out to be as I suspected. She was cordial and businesslike as we hammered out the fine points of payment for, and distribution of, the new flyers. Like the previous ones, they were eye-watering in their intensity, like the progeny of a haz-mat sign and crime-scene bunting. I couldn't honestly say I liked them, but there was no disputing their power to arrest the eye and keep it overnight for questioning. I handed over some money and got Cheyenne's assurance that she would have the city plastered in flyers by Wednesday.

I proceeded to tick off a major portion of the items on my must-do list, including putting a deposit on my tuxedo, arranging for the delivery of the kegs, buying cups, finalizing the details for the porta-johns, and hiring a light and sound crew to manage the technical wizardry that every successful band needs to satisfy today's discriminating audience.

By the time I headed back to Dudleigh, I had only a couple of gaps in my strategy for preparedness. I hadn't yet decided how to handle the collection of fees at the door, and I wanted to find someone trustworthy to oversee the beer sales. I had plenty of friends who would volunteer. But few, if any of them, could be described as completely trustworthy when the subject is beer. I thought it might be best to bring in someone from outside the family, so to speak, to man the tap with a clear eye and a cool head. But who?

Had it not been Monday, I might have stopped by Antiqua for a spot of managerial advice from HarLar, but I recalled that he was closed on my day off. I was drawing a blank, and it was that quiet point in the afternoon when the busy lunch hour has turned the corner toward the dinner shift but hasn't yet gotten up to speed, when I had a sudden inspiration and pulled into the café lot. I hurried in the back door, hoping to avoid Glory out of general principles, and came upon the very person I wanted to see.

Marilyn Rider was wiping down the bar, with the kind of vigorous motion that casts a hypnotic spell on all the boys who frequent the place. Her luxuriant hair was swept up in a kind of messy pile of curls, one of which dangled loose down the front of her low-cut blouse. I shook myself and said, "Hey Marilyn, are you busy Saturday night?"

She rolled her eyes and said, "What do you think?"

Duh. Of course she was busy, every Saturday night, and if she weren't, Eduardo would want her all to himself. So the chance of her being willing to work as my keg master was zip. But as long as I was there, I asked if she knew anyone who might be good for the job.

"You're going to pay them right?" she asked.

I hadn't thought it through, really, but now that she mentioned it, I realized that it might be one way to ensure a certain level of responsibility. "Sure. Of course," I said.

"You should ask Marcy. She's off Saturday nights. She might do it for the money."

As soon as she said it, I realized how perfect Marcy would be. Those motorcycle boots sort of send a message, you know? I hastened to the kitchen to sound her out.

"How much?" she asked, after I'd sketched the essentials.

"You mean, how much money will you get?"

"Uh, huh."

"How does fifty bucks sound?"

She grimaced. "How long do you want me to pump beer? Two hours?"

"Um. No. It might be more like four." I could see she wasn't overly thrilled at the prospect. "All right, how about a hundred?"

She shrugged. "Okay, I guess. Can I bring somebody to help me?"

"Sure."

"And you can pay them fifty bucks."

I sighed. What could I say? It wasn't unreasonable. If there were hundreds of people jamming up to get beer it would be prudent to have more than one person. "That's fine," I said.

"Okay then. What time you want us there?"

I told myself this was all to the good. Another item crossed off the old list. That left only the really sticky one, and I was beginning to realize that when it all came down, I was going to have to do it. Nobody I knew would be willing to take the money at the door. Or, let me qualify that. Nobody I trusted to handle a large sum of money on which my whole future depended. I couldn't afford to take a chance on Photon, or Randall, or even Eric, in his girlfriend-besotted state. I needed someone whom I could count on to stay sober and vigilant until the last paying customer had coughed up. And then there was the problem of what to do with all that cash until I could turn it over to the thug brothers. Just thinking about having that much money on me made me a little nervous. I wouldn't even be able to get stoned.

As the significance of this dawned on me, I came to the dreary conclusion that, not only was Jenny not going to be there, and not only was I going to have to miss most of the biggest party of my life, but I was going to have to stay straight for the entire night. What a bummer.

A dark mood had me in its grip as I drove back to the shack. If this is what it took to be a successful manager, maybe it wasn't the career choice for me after all. But, I couldn't bail on the concert. I was in too deep. I had to just suck it up and hope that I at least broke even at the end of the day. I'd lost track of how much money I'd been throwing around. And what if only a couple hundred people showed up? It could be a disaster.

If only Jenny were going to be there, I wouldn't care if I lost every cent, if that's what it took to make her change her mind and stay. But now I couldn't even hope for that.

Back at the shack I sat in the truck for half a minute, trying to see a bright side in the gloom. After all, some good might still come of all of this. *Virtus vincit omnia*, as the fellow said. Virtue conquers all things.

I stepped out and immediately noticed that the air had changed since morning. There was a kind of edge to it, as if the gods were snapping towels at the trees. The air was full of the sound of leaves skittering along the ground and rattling against the branches. A bit on the ominous side. I had a sudden recollection of other autumns, when the normal seasonal zest took a turn for the psychotic, thanks to some tropical storm veering inland for a bit of off-season mayhem. It wouldn't help the turnout Saturday if the weather went all King Learish. I trudged to the shack in a state of glum resignation. Fine, I thought. Blow wind and crack thy ruddy cheeks if you must. But get it over with before Saturday.

Unfortunately, by the next morning, what had appeared to be a passing bluster turned into a full-fledged storm system, which parked itself in our faire realm for the next three days, soaking one and all and smashing the bright leaves to a sodden brown carpet. Business came to a halt at the café. We sat around and played cards in the kitchen to pass the time in the afternoon, while Glory stalked around like a jilted bride, glaring out the windows at the empty parking lot.

I tried not to think what effect this soggy shut-in scenario might be having on the band. One could only hope they weren't getting on each other's nerves, tactlessly pointing out minor character flaws and personal failings. Maybe they had worked out all their little differences and were even now polishing up some rocking new songs for the concert. I didn't believe this for a minute, but the important thing with delusions is that they fill up the space that could otherwise be taken over by anxiety. I prefer to dream bright dreams of platinum instead.

Late Thursday afternoon these dreams were put on hold by a call from Delilah. My spirits, low already, slunk deeper at the sound of her voice. It was sharp as a bandsaw.

"Hey Manager. Haven't seen you for a while."

"Ah, Delilah. How's it going? Matt's back, right? You guys all ready for the big night?" Mr. Upbeat could take my correspondence course.

A chunk of silence broke off and drifted down the phone line like an iceberg. "Ahem," I continued, "I've been meaning to call and let you know how things are going. I've been pretty busy getting everything lined up for the concert."

Again with the silence.

"Um, is everything all right over there?" I asked, sticking a reluctant toe in the frigid pool.

"Oh sure," she said. "Everything's just peachy here. Tucker's not too happy with you, though. And Matt hasn't come out of his room since he got back. Crater's starting to fidget, and that's never a good sign."

I took all of this under advisement, but refused to give in to the Dark Side. "How about Jimmy? How's he holding up? And Denny? He's all right, I bet."

She sniffed. "Oh those two. They're the same as ever. They just want to play all the time."

As she mentioned this, I noticed that in the background I could hear a guitar and keyboard having a desultory musical conversation, as if the topic were faithless women and the men who love them. Sort of heartwarming, really.

"Well that's good isn't it? I mean, with all this rain, you might as well stay inside and write songs, right?"

"That's easy for you to say."

"Yes. Well. I'm just the manager. I make no claim to fully understand the creative process—"

"Can it, Moon! This isn't a social call. I've seen this kind of thing before and I know the signs. This band is one hissy-fit away from a complete melt-down. If you think you can do anything to fix it, you'd better do it fast, or there won't be any band left for your precious concert."

Oh hell. "I'm on my way," I said. But not with any enthusiasm. No. I think it's safe to say that by this time my enthusiasm had been more or less hit by a truck, run over, and left at the side of the road to be pecked by buzzards. And all I could say was, *bon appetit.*

Driving through the monsoon to the band's house, I wracked the brain for ideas to restore harmony. The irony of the quest was not lost upon me, but I felt that the band was probably not attuned to irony. Hah. I couldn't help myself. The old Moon resilience was back in business.

As I neared the scene of conflict, I found myself remembering other, brighter days of dramatic challenges, when I was tested and not found wanting during many a grueling certamen event. While others about me grappled with little known details of Roman life and history, or were bested by the minutia of Latin grammar, I strode among them like a giant, confident, untouchable, yet as gracious in victory as I no doubt would have been in defeat, if I'd ever been defeated. Which, ahem, I wasn't. This was the state of mind I needed, I realized with a sudden flash of insight, if I were ever to gain the upper hand over these scruffy, ego-driven rockers. My mistake had been allowing them to imagine themselves superior to me on the flimsy premise that they were somehow extraordinarily gifted by Euterpe herself. Hah. I'll bet they didn't even have a clue who she was.

The key, I suddenly realized, was to be above it all. I had allowed them to believe that I was needy. And, I suppose if I'm being honest with myself, I was a bit needy at first. But now... I don't know why... maybe it's the cumulative effect of all this damned rain and the constant bludgeoning of fate, but I no longer cared what they thought of me. I knew my worth. But I wasn't so sure about theirs anymore.

As I stepped out of the truck and into a puddle up to my shin, I thought to myself that these motley musicians had better watch their step. There are worse things than puddles. I shook my wet shoe and trotted up onto the porch, where all the dogs were huddled. Their tails thumped with hope at the sight of me. Perhaps they thought I'd let them in. I considered this as I waited for someone to open the door. And then it came to me.

I opened the door and let them all in with me.

"Hey! Don't let those damned wet dogs in here!"

I looked across the room to see who had said this. Crater glared at me from the couch. I gazed coolly back at him and said, "These dogs deserve better treatment."

Crater stared at me, his mouth hanging open. I looked around the room and saw that Jimmy and Denny were still at their instruments, playing quietly. There was no sign of Tucker or Matt. Delilah entered, stage left, put her hands on her hips and said, "That was quick."

I looked pointedly at Crater and said, "We need to talk."

He scowled at me and turned away. I turned to Delilah and said, "Get Matt and Tucker in here. I don't want to have to say this twice."

She raised an eyebrow, but she didn't argue. She went out of the room and I heard her knocking on a door and some rapid back and forth. I waited where I was, standing at the edge of the room with the dogs sitting in rapt attention at my feet. They can spot an alpha male when they see one.

After a few minutes, Matt came slouching out from the hall. He gave me a look of mild contempt before dropping into an overstuffed chair. I could hear Delilah shouting at Tucker upstairs. Eventually the shouting stopped. She appeared and said, "He'll be right down."

I waited, still silent, gathering my forces.

When Tucker finally shuffled down the stairs, the mood in the room had subtly altered. The other members of the band may not have been aware of my sly strategy, but inevitably, as they were forced to wait upon their lead singer, the focus of their irritation shifted from me to him. He was the prima donna. Not me.

However, I came not to harrie Caesar but to braise him. Hah. Once I get going, it's hard to stop myself. And why should I?

"Why do some bands succeed while others fail?" I knew this was like throwing a match on a pool of gasoline, and, as expected, Crater, Tucker and Matt exploded simultaneously with derision.

"Why is this clown even here?" Tucker complained.

I turned to Delilah. "Do you want to tell him or shall I?"

She was looking at me with a mask of calm, but I detected an amused curiosity in her eyes. "You go ahead, Manager."

I turned back to the boys and said, "It's not a question of talent," I allowed my gaze to rest on Jimmy and Denny, "or charisma," a nod to Matt, "or looks," a glance at Tucker. "The reason some bands succeed, even bands who lack the kind of talent, charisma and looks that this band has, is that they work together, and they stay together, and they commit to the process."

"And they get lucky." I didn't recognize the voice, and at first I actually looked down at the dogs before I realized that Jimmy, the Silent One, had spoken.

His words drew a murmur of agreement from the rest. I took this as a good sign. At least they agreed on something.

"Luck is a part of life. But a wise man once said, 'The harder I try, the luckier I get.' And that's something this band hasn't accepted yet. Up to now, you've had some success, here in the backwoods where there's not much competition. But if you hope to make a name for yourselves out there, out in the larger world, you're going to have to put some effort into it. You're going to have to do some things you don't want to. You're going to have to work."

"Work?" cracked Denny, in a voice like Maynard G. Krebs.

I acknowledged this Dobie Gillis reference with a slight smile. You have to respect the classics, even the ones that aren't in Latin.

"I know some of you aren't very excited about this concert Saturday. Maybe you think it's stupid. Maybe you think it's a waste of time. But here's the bottom line: I'm expecting a crowd of five hundred people to pay ten dollars each to hear you play, and, after expenses, that works out to at least a thousand dollars for the band.

Maybe more. That's not a fortune, but it's more than you're going to make diddling around in your living room or jamming in some hole-in-the-wall club. It's an opportunity to expand your fan base and deliver a good show. You're lucky to get the chance to do it. If you don't get that... then maybe you should quit right now, and I'll find another band that wants a chance to make it." I looked around the room quietly, making eye contact with each one of them. "Any one of those bands that played at that Battle of the Bands in Charlottesville—you think they wouldn't jump at the chance?"

I let that hang in the air. No one said anything for a minute. Then Delilah straightened up and said, "I want to do this gig. Anyone who doesn't... can leave now."

No one moved. They didn't look at me. They didn't have to. The rules had changed.

When it was clear to everyone that we were going ahead, I decided to make a gesture, to show I still believed in them.

"I know some of you are probably not too keen on the idea of wearing costumes for this gig, and if you really feel strongly about it, you don't have to. It's strictly optional. But I'll tell you this. I know from experience that when you go to a costume party, and everyone there is in costume, and you're not, you'll wish you were. It doesn't have to be much. A cowboy hat, a fake beard. You'll have more fun. I guarantee."

The guys shifted in their seats, but no one said anything except Matt who muttered, "No way in hell."

"I'll tell you what," I said, feeling the divine spark of inspiration. "I'll give fifty bucks to anyone who wants to rent a costume."

"Cool," said Crater. "I'm in."

Tucker frowned. "Where's this fifty bucks coming from? Out of our profits?"

I shook my head. "No. This is from me to you. If it will encourage anyone to get into the spirit, it's worth fifty bucks to me."

"Hell, I'll take fifty bucks. I can just get myself a cowboy hat, right?" Tucker smirked at me as if he'd figured out a way to cheat on a test. He just didn't get it.

"Sure," I said. "Whatever puts you in the mood. I want you guys to have fun Saturday. It could be a great night."

Delilah was smiling by this time. She held her hand out. "Okay, Manager. I'll see what I can come up with for fifty bucks."

In the end, they all took the money, which cleaned me out. And I suppose I knew that I was being taken advantage of. But you have to give to receive. Besides, at this point it wasn't about making money, for me. If it ever was. It was always about Jenny. And that hope was gone. I might as well try to make it a good time for everyone else. It was the least I could do.

CHAPTER TWENTY

Sona si laitine loqueris
Honk if you speak Latin.

The following morning a brighter sun burnished the new day. Maybe it felt so to me because of my triumph over the troglodytes the evening before. But I think my uplift was due more to the fact that when I returned to the shack last night, I didn't fall into a morose stupor, dwelling on the sadness of life and the inevitability of death and whatnot. Instead, inspired by the empowering influence of the classics, I pulled out my old copy of H.A. Guerber's "The Myths of Greece and Rome" and spent a few soothing hours being reminded of what tough times those ancient Greeks and Romans had of it, with vengeful scheming gods and muses constantly chaining them to rocks or transforming them into trees or whatever. Rape, murder, incest, and spiteful torture were all in a day's work for the average deity back in those days. Kind of put my own little problems in perspective.

Perspective, I told myself, as I drifted into a pleasant, dreamless sleep, was the real key to happiness. What did it matter, in the big scheme of things, after all, if I lost every cent and the woman I love, and ended up alone and heartbroken again? At least I was reasonably sure that I wouldn't be transformed into a swan or something.

With this brave new outlook, I went back to work that Friday, firm in the conviction that in this life about all you can do, really, is keep your chin up and be alert for thunderbolts.

As I passed through the kitchen, Glory told me to stop whistling. I shrugged it off. Her lack of musical appreciation is well known.

Midway through the day Phoebe called, all aflutter because she and her crew of volunteers were hoping to get into the Hangar today to start putting up the decorations, but a snag had arisen, or fallen, technically, in the form of a huge pine tree which had apparently come unmoored during the three-day rain. The tree now lay across the narrow gravel road that leads to the Hangar, thus blocking all access. I smiled grimly, sensing the work of some god with too much time on his hands. I told Phoebe not to fret and that I would take care of it. However, after I hung up, I realized that I had no phone number for the owner. I would have to drive there, climb over the tree, hike to the Hangar, or to the old guy's house back in the cow field, and hope that he had a chainsaw. Or...

"This better be good," Witty growled. Normally I never call him at work. When he gets to hammering, he unleashes the floodgates that ordinarily hold his testosterone at bay, and it takes him a while to remember who his friends are.

"I wouldn't call if it weren't an emergency," I said quickly. "You have a chainsaw."

"A lot of guys have chainsaws, Duggie. Whyn't you call one of them?"

"Because I thought you wanted Delilah to be happy."

I could almost hear the gears shifting in his brain. They were grinding a little, but that was to be expected. "What's she got to do with this?"

Quickly, in words of one syllable, I explained the scenario: tree fall; road blocked; gig not... well, okay, I branched out into longer words once it became clear he was paying attention. He grumbled a little, but he agreed to meet me at the entrance to the Hangar drive in half an hour. I called Phoebe back and told her help was on the way. She squeaked with delight and called me her hero. I saw no reason to correct her. Girls enjoy their little fantasies. Who was I to deny Phoebe hers?

When we arrived at the scene of the tree, Phoebe and three other lissome young women sprang out of her car and stood around eyeing Witty as he strode up with the chainsaw. I could tell he noticed them by how hard he was pretending not to.

He walked back and forth along the length of the tree, taking in its girth. Then he frowned slightly and cranked up the chainsaw. The girls all covered their ears and stepped back. I wanted to cover my ears, but I didn't want to seem like a wuss. Witty was bare-eared, his biceps gleaming in the sunlight flickering between the trees.

It didn't take him long to cut the trunk into sections. Then we had to get them off the road. I felt I had to step up for this task, especially since a couple of the girls were jumping forward to lend a hand. But Witty waved them off and said, "There's no need for you girls to mess up your nice clothes. These logs are gonna be messy. They're full of sap."

I resisted the urge to add a quip here, feeling that it wouldn't be fair to mock Witt when he'd come to my aid. I also didn't want to undermine the impression he'd made on Phoebe's pals, since, although his heart currently belonged to Delilah, I knew only too well that a post-Delilah era was inevitable, and it wouldn't hurt to have some candidates already selected for the next bout.

When he'd cleared the drive, Phoebe dashed forward and threw her arms around him, in her impulsive way, and gushed, "You're my hero!"

The twinge of jealousy I felt took me by surprise, but I quickly smothered it. After all, I had no right to stop this open-hearted girl from sharing her affections with anyone she chose. I guess I was so used to feeling that I, and I alone, was her hero that it kind of brought me up short to hear her apply the term to someone else. I shook it off and smiled as the other three girls joined Phoebe in a group hug centered on Witty that brought the bright flush of embarrassment to his face. He sort of shrugged loose of them after a few seconds and mumbled, "It was nothing." Then he turned to me and said, "I gotta go back to work." He got in his truck and glanced back at the girls, who were all smiling and waving at him. He waved back with a little smile and drove off.

Phoebe skipped over to me then and asked if I wanted to come and help decorate the Hangar, as long as I was there. I was tempted. Glory was already giving me Saturday off. She'd go ballistic if I didn't show up for the dinner shift. But I figured I had a few hours to spare.

So I followed the girls to the Hangar, and it's a good thing I did. The place looked and smelled exactly as it had the last time I was there. In other words, like a garage which hadn't been cleaned in decades. I glanced at the pep squad and saw their foreheads pucker with frowny lines. But girls like these are nothing if not plucky. Some might even say spunky, but I've never really cottoned to that term. Still, call it what you will, there's no question that these girls didn't shy away from a challenge that would have daunted Martha Stewart. They hustled into action, sweeping, cleaning, organizing. Then, once they'd established a perimeter, they scrambled up ladders, tacked up the parachutes, hung a mirror ball and a few glow-in-the-dark skeletons. By the time I had to go back to work, the place was starting to look downright festive, and I was feeling that things might just work out for once.

I pointedly ignored the little snicker I thought I heard in the ether. Probably just some delinquent deity looking to bring me down. Bring it on, punk, I thought. *Fabricati diem*. Make my day.

Well, you know how in the movies they have those montages where everything kind of slows down, and you see how all the little details mount up to create the Big Picture? The rest of that day and the start of Saturday weren't like that. I felt as if I were clinging to a runaway train, and it was roaring past all the stops where I had thought I'd have time to jump out and buy a paper or a snack. Friday night was a blur. Saturday the start gun went bang, and I was off, picking up my costume, overseeing the installation of the porta-johns, setting up tables, and helping the sound and lighting guys find what they needed.

By late in the afternoon, I was starting to run out of gas and wondering if I dared to sneak back to the shack for a quiet toke or two before the main event. But then my phone started ringing, people asking for directions, people asking if they could get in free, people asking if there was a costume contest. I began to wish I had a secretary.

And even as all this was going on, the clock kept ticking. The one good thing about being too busy to think is that it kept me from dwelling on how the one person I wanted to see more than any other on this night wouldn't be there.

As night fell it looked like everything was as ready as it was going to be. Phoebe and her girls had brought in a wagon load of pumpkins to put the finishing touch on the decor. I warned them to limit the number of candles, hoping to avoid a repeat of the tent fiasco. Marcie arrived with her friend, a tall brooding sort of girl with a shaved head and a spiked collar. Just what the doctor ordered.

As I slipped into my tux in a dark corner behind the stage area, I began to feel just a bit edgy about the band. I'd told them they should be ready to start playing by about eight thirty, but I was beginning to wish I'd thought of arranging for an opening act to cover the awkward interim as people were arriving, before the band took the stage. When I stepped out of the shadows into the lighted area, I heard a gasp and looked around. Phoebe was staring at me with the old lovelight on high beam. I smiled. She shook her head and came over to me and said, "Oh Duggie. You look wonderful!"

She was dressed in a kind of Tinkerbell motif. It suited her. She looked adorable. I told her so, and she responded by hugging me with a warmth that I have to say was comforting. It's just too bad she's not the right girl for me.

I headed out to the front to take my place at the door. I had a cash box, some change, and a chair in case I got tired of standing. Photon was going to serve as my muscle, to stop any deadbeats who tried to sneak past me. But we both knew that he wouldn't be able to resist the call of the revels once they got going. Still, I appreciated any help I could get. I had asked Randall to be my backup guy, but he declined, saying he had a day job. Well, so have I, I could have said, but I didn't blame him. Basically I'd accepted the fact that this concert wasn't for me. It was a party for everyone else. And all I really wanted was for them to have a great time.

The paying customers started rolling in around eight o'clock. For the first twenty minutes or so, the incoming rate was a bit less than I'd hoped, but they all seemed in high spirits, and at least half of them were in costume, the girls tending to more elaborate efforts than the guys for the most part. Except for one guy who appeared in an over-the-top King Tut outfit. He waved the flyer at me as he handed me his money and asked, "What's the prize?"

I was stumped. I looked at the flyer, which was the second version, and noticed for the first time that in bold neon print at the bottom it said, "Costume contest! Cash prizes!"

I sighed inwardly. Too late to worry about it now.

"How much?" Tut asked. His royal outfit must have set him back. No doubt he was hoping to break even.

"A hundred dollars for first place," I said. Maybe I'd have that much to spare when this was all over.

The king nodded and said, "Shweet!"

By eight thirty, there was still no sign of anyone from the band, although they'd come over earlier in the afternoon to set up their equipment. But before I had a chance to get a full-scale panic going, a wiry pirate with a fake parrot on his shoulder poked me with a cutlass, and I recognized Crater under his bandana.

"Arrrh. Ya ready to parrrty, mate?" he said.

"Won't that sword won't get in the way of your drumming?"

"Nah. Might work it into the act." He flashed a grin and went in.

Behind him, Denny sauntered past, wearing a purple and white Cat in the Hat top hat. I clutched at his jacket as he went by and asked if he could play some instrumentals to keep the crowd happy until the whole band got there. He shrugged and said, "Sure. That's what I'm here for."

I sighed with satisfaction. If only they were all as easy-going and professional as Denny, I could almost consider doing this seriously.

A moment later, Tucker swaggered up, wearing a cowboy hat, tight jeans, and a vest with no shirt on under it. Mr. Minimum Effort. "Nice to see you Tucker," I said, wearing the mask.

He gave me a look that would have said volumes if he had a more extensive vocabulary. As it was, he managed to convey his habitual juvenile contempt. I sighed again. But Tucker's tiresome routine vanished from my thoughts at the sight of Delilah.

A fairly sizable crowd had arrived by this time, and they were pressing around the door waiting to get in, but they parted like the Red Sea to watch Delilah glide through in her sensational Cleopatra get-up. She had the hair-do, the eye-makeup, the cleavage. She was carrying a scepter and trailing some kind of exotic scent. Her earrings and bangles chinked like tossed coins as she walked. Mouths hung open in her wake.

"Wow," I said, speaking for the multitude.

She smiled. "You like?"

Several voices in the crowd responded with resounding "Whoo-whoos." She looked over her shoulder at the mob and tossed a sultry smile, then vanished inside. The crowd closed in on me, pressing money in my face.

There was a scuffle of sorts and the sound of people complaining about feet being stepped on, and then Witty strode to the front barking, "Let me through."

I have to say, he'd outdone himself. Obviously he was taking his new role as a bodyguard seriously. From the tip of his feathered helmet to the leather straps of his centurion sandals, he looked every inch a gladiator. His metal breastplate was dented as with battle scars, and only a fool with a death wish would have the nerve to mock the bare knees showing below his Roman kirtle.

"I'm with the band," he grumbled, shooting a warning look at me. I wasn't about to poke the bear. I nodded and said, "She's right inside."

I barely noticed when Jimmy and Matt slipped by me. They were both wearing black. Big surprise. Cheyenne was trailing behind Matt, though, and she had some sort of Vampyra outfit on, low-cut and clingy.

From that point on, I was gathering money so fast I had to wad some of it in my coat pockets; it was too much to hold and I didn't have time to mess with the cash box. On the one hand, this was great. I had no idea how much we'd made so far, but it had to be almost enough to pay back the thugs, and that was the only part I was really concerned about. If the band didn't make a fortune tonight, they'd survive.

I started to relax when I heard the opening chords of "Jump To It," their signature dance tune. Glancing inside, I could see the crowd was already gyrating with a will. The scent of spilled beer was beginning to make itself noticed, along with an undercurrent of another familiar fragrance. I felt a pang of envy. I could almost be having fun if I didn't have to be the grown-up at this event. Another reason I'm not cut out for this managerial role.

Still, it was a beautiful night. The air was brisk. The sky was clear, radiant with stars, et cetera. If I'd had my girl at my side it would be paradise enow, as the fellow said. However, guests were still trickling in, in waves, which was good, because it kept me from getting too maudlin. A rowdy bunch showed up around ten and tried to argue that they should be let in for half price, since the event was half over. I could have disputed this on mathematical grounds, but something told me that the guy in the wizard hat who was the most insistent in the group had not actually done his homework. Eventually they gave up and paid with a hundred dollar bill, which I had my doubts about, but the light wasn't good enough to examine it so I had to take it on faith.

The batch behind them was less obnoxious and included a fairly authentic Zorro, a Harpo with an aoogah horn, and an Indiana Jones with a bullwhip. He assured me he didn't know how to use it.

Then things got really busy again, and I was taking money so fast that I hardly looked up to see who or what was handing it to me, until maybe around eleven when a hand reached out and grabbed my arm as I was about to stuff some more bills in my jacket. I looked up and saw Elvis.

"Good evening, Mr. Moon." He lifted his mask and I stared into the chiseled features of one of the thugs. "Is Goran. And you remember Nikolai," he said, gesturing at his partner, who looked completely incongruous in a regulation Star Trek uniform. He was wearing Spock ears, but he hadn't gone as far as the green skin. Some people just won't make the effort.

"Oh. I didn't expect to see you guys here tonight."

Elvis shrugged. "We think, maybe we kill two birds with one rock, no? You have the money now, yes? We get the money. We hear your band. Everybody's happy."

I thought about it. It would be great to get some of this money off my hands. It was so much I was kind of worried about carrying it around. "I guess that would be okay. You'll give me a receipt, right?"

"Of course. We give you receipt. We mark it paid. Everything legit."

"Okay. I need to get someone to watch the door while I count it out."

"Nikolai."

I glanced at the mock Spock. Then I figured, what the hell. "Okay."

Goran and I stepped away from the door, and I counted out the money. When I got to three thousand I handed it to him. Then he said, "And six hundred."

"Right." I counted out the interest. He handed me a receipt. We shook hands.

"Pleasure doing business with you," he said. Then he turned to Nikolai and said, "We go in now." He peeled off two tens to give me. I shook my head.

"You guys go in as my guests. I couldn't have done it without you." And strange as it may seem, at that moment I had a kind of warm feeling of gratitude. Veiled threats aside, these two had been cordial and businesslike throughout our brief encounters, and as a businessman, I appreciated that.

I watched them wander into the clamorous crowd and felt the weight lifting from my shoulders. My debt was paid. Whatever happened now, all the money I had left in my pockets could go to the band. And the costume contest. Speaking of which, I wondered when that event was going to take place. It occurred to me that the band might not realize that someone had to take charge and make it happen. And who better than I?

The influx of guests had slowed to a trickle at this late hour. Perhaps I could safely abandon my post and join the party. After another moment of hesitation, I realized this was my choice to make. It was my party, after all.

I squared my shoulders and headed into the throng.

As I got closer to the stage, I sensed that the momentum of the evening had taken a strange detour into the combat zone.

The band wasn't exactly playing a song at the moment, though Denny and Jimmy were keeping up a kind of crisp musical dialogue, like a tango without the dancing, and out front in the lights it appeared that Matt and Delilah were having a heated discussion. I couldn't hear what they were saying, but as I came in range I saw Delilah turn toward Witty, who was looming behind her like an angry troll, and I heard her scream, "Are you going to let him talk to me like that?"

Witty lurched into action, brandishing his sword at Matt, who was unarmed and took a step behind Tucker. Tucker sneered at Witty and said, "Put that thing away before you hurt somebody."

I could have told Tucker that Witty doesn't respond well to being told what to do, but I felt that perhaps there are some lessons lead singers have to learn on their own. Witty took another step closer to Tucker and touched him on the chest with the point of his sword. "You better watch your mouth," he growled.

At this point most everyone in the room was watching this show, and I felt that it might be best to step in before chaos erupted. I pushed forward and climbed onto the stage, but not before Crater had leapt out from behind his drum set with his cutlass glinting in the spotlights.

"Step back, Tucker," he said. "I'll handle this goon."

I moved in front of them then, trying to block the audience's view. I held up my hands and said, "Don't worry folks. It's all part of the show. A little Halloween high jinks to get you in the mood for the costume contest." I clapped enthusiastically and turned around and glared at the boys with swords, and said sotto voce, "Cut it out. Now."

They lowered their weapons but remained facing each other, neither one willing to back down.

"Come on now, ladies and gentlemen. Who's got the best costume here tonight?" I said. "Anyone who thinks they've got the best costume, come on up here and we'll let the audience vote."

There was some movement in the crowd, and within a few minutes a half dozen characters were preening in the lights. Reading from left to right they were: a girl dressed as Raggedy Ann, a guy dressed as a giant bottle of tequila with a rather grotesque worm attached to his head, a Samurai in the manner of John Belushi, the King Tut guy, a huge chicken, and a girl dressed as Wonder Woman.

It was a tough field, though if it were up to me, I'd toss out the Raggedy Ann and the Samurai to start with, for lack of imagination, but I left it to the crowd, asking them to applaud for their favorite as I called out each one's name. It was pretty clear that it was between King Tut and Wonder Woman, though the tequila bottle had a strong following. Every time I put the spotlight on him, he did a funny little tap dance routine that drew howls from the fans. Once we'd narrowed it down to two candidates, I asked the audience to cheer for their favorite. It was loud. So loud that at first I didn't notice the resumption of hostilities behind me, until Matt went sailing over my head and landed on top of the crowd pressed up against the stage, who fortunately broke his fall. I turned around in time to see Tucker punching Witty in the back, while Witt had his hands full parrying Crater's slashing cutlass.

I yelled at them to stop, but my screams were lost in the general din. Denny and Jimmy were still playing, thank god, but Delilah was nowhere in sight. I was actually glad to see she'd had the sense to get away from the melee. But some people love a good brawl.

The tequila bottle apparently was one of those. Perhaps being encased in a sturdy cardboard suit, he felt he could take a few swings at King Tut, whose regal attitude was rubbing some the wrong way. And the giant chicken joined in, jabbing at anyone who came within pecking distance. Even Raggedy Ann, who one might have thought would be a peaceful soul, was making the most of the moment by pulling Wonder Woman's hair. Wonder Woman responded with a solid punch that decked the doll.

All in all, it's safe to say that the situation was out of control. Yet, in the midst of all the turmoil, I was surprised as I crept toward the edge of the stage to hear the rhythm section kick in. I looked back and saw Elvis playing the drums, while Nikolai took over the bass. Jimmy and Denny never missed a beat. People out in the crowd were dancing, oblivious.

As I worked my way toward the door, I was overcome by an apocalyptic sense of finality. So this is it, I was thinking—the band finished, Jenny gone, no money to my name. Judging by the violence taking place on all sides, I'd be lucky if I didn't get sued.

I ran into Photon, boogying hard. Looking around the room, I wondered how it would all end. If it would all end. I wondered if I had to stay until they'd all gone. I caught Photon's bloodshot eye and yelled, "How do I get them to leave?"

"Don't worry. When the kegs run out, they'll go," he roared back.

"How long will that take?" I asked.

"I'm on it," he said, and lumbered off.

As I picked my way across the floor littered with empty cups, feathers and glitter, I shuddered to think what a mess the parking field would be once all these people started trying to get out. I was keeping my head down, concentrating on not falling down, when I bumped into someone. I looked up and saw that it was an angel. A blonde angel. How nice, I thought. And then I looked closer. The angel had tears on her face. I stared. She looked strangely familiar. And she was looking at me as if... suddenly my arms were around her.

"Jenny," I whispered.

"Oh Duggie. Take me home."

CHAPTER TWENTY-ONE

Felix qui potuit rerum cognoscere causas
Fortunate is he who has been able to learn the causes of things.
Virgil

I grabbed her hand, and we started for the door, but before we reached it, I felt the clutch of another hand on my jacket. I started to shrug off whoever it was, but then I saw it was King Tut himself.

"Hey, man. Do I get the money? I won, didn't I?"

I reached inside my jacket, pulled out a wad of bills, peeled off five twenties and handed it to him. He beamed and said, "Thanks, man! Great party! Happy Halloween!" and vanished back into the hive.

Jenny was staring at me and my wad o' cash. I shrugged. "It's not as much as it looks. I haven't paid the band yet."

She smiled at me, and I felt like a millionaire. I wrapped an arm around her shoulders, which wasn't as easy as you might think, because she had these feathery wings attached to her costume, and we started off to my truck. Since she had stopped crying, I thought it might be safe to ask what had brought on the tears, but I was afraid to break the happy spell of the moment. Still, I wasn't sure where she wanted me to take her. Did she mean home as in where she had been living for the last month? Or... home with me?

As soon as we got in the truck, she turned to me and said, "I've been so stupid. Can you forgive me?"

"You've never been stupid in your life. I'm the stupid one."

She shook her head, and for a second I worried that she was going to start crying again, but she kind of pressed her lips together and seemed to be trembling, and suddenly I recognized the rare but unmistakable signs of her anger. She was pissed! But not at me! This night just kept getting better!

"I should have known," she said, in a low, thrilling tone. "When he told me about this so-called 'thing' he had to go to tonight, all of a sudden, after he'd been so eager to hear your band again, you know? But I just swallowed it. His whole 'I'm so sorry' crap. And all the time..." She took a few deep breaths and seemed to struggle to get a grip.

"You mean Miles?"

"Hunh. Who else? And I would never have known if it weren't for Morris. He's the real angel."

I gaped at her, not able to picture it. "Morris had something to do with this?"

"He's the reason I'm here."

"What? Is he here? I didn't see him."

"No. He just dropped me off. He said he couldn't stand to be in big noisy crowds anymore. But... I was at home, finishing up the packing for Paris—what a dope—and there was a knock at the door, and it was Morris, and I was, like, what are you doing here? And he said he'd heard about how I wasn't going to be able to come to the concert, and he said he had a meeting in D.C. earlier today, and he thought maybe if I wanted, he could give me a ride to the concert."

"That doesn't sound like him."

"I know. I should have realized it was more than coincidence when he handed me the costume."

"He got you a costume?"

She gestured at the white satin gown, which fit her like... wait, I missed something—

"—and he said he got me the blonde wig, because he thought it would be more fun to surprise you."

"Wow. Yeah. But I knew it was you as soon as I looked in your eyes."

"Un, huh? When I handed you my ten bucks, you didn't even look up."

"I had my hands full."

She frowned and looked away. I wondered if I'd said the wrong thing. But then she continued, gazing out the window, and her voice took on this kind of hard glittering edge.

"Yeah. You weren't the only one. I was walking around enjoying the concert. And then the fighting started, and that was entertaining too, in its own way." She shook her head and smiled at me for a second. "Witty with that sword! I'm glad I got to see that." Then she shelved the smile and said, "But after a few minutes, I had this funny feeling. I don't know why. Like, there was something I needed to do? And I walked around by the side of the stage, and that's when I saw him."

"Who?"

"Zorro. With his hands all over Cleopatra."

I blinked. "Who with what?"

"Zorro—Miles! Groping your singer. And she was groping back."

The mental picture snapped into focus. Miles and Delilah. Of course! Now that she paired their names, I realized it was probably inevitable. Like two highly charged particles combusting when they come in contact.

"I should have figured it out weeks ago. Ever since he saw her at that wedding, he's been mentioning the band, kind of casually. Too casually, you know? But I'm such a fool, I never saw it coming."

I wanted to wrap my arms around her and kiss away the tears, but she wasn't crying anymore. She was boiling mad. She reached out and took my hand and pulled me close and said, "I'm so sorry, Duggie. I got so dazzled by the whole 'going to Paris, hanging out with artists' crap. And the truth is, Miles and his whole world can't touch you. You're the coolest. This whole party? The way you did all this work so everyone could have a great night? That's so you. I just love that about you."

Well, I was glowing. Who wouldn't in the face of such praise? And best of all, it was Jenny saying these things.

I could have sat there happily for the rest of my life, I think. It was so perfect. The moon, the stars, Jenny's face shining at me brighter than either of them.

There was a tap at the window. Of course. Perfection can't last. I turned irritably and saw Vampyra lurking in the darkness. I sighed and rolled down the window.

"Are you leaving?" she demanded.

"Yes."

"Matt wants his money."

I noticed then another dark shape lurking behind her. "I haven't counted it up yet. I don't know how much—"

"Give him two hundred, and we'll leave you alone."

I considered this. It might be more than he was worth, seeing as how he'd quit before the end. But then, perhaps that hadn't been entirely his fault. I pulled out the good old wad once again and counted out the sum and handed it to her. "Happy Halloween," I said.

She shook her head at me. "You're pathetic."

I felt this was uncalled for, but I let it slide. No doubt she had problems of her own. I rolled the window back up and turned to Jenny. She was grinning at me, like old times.

"So, do you want me to give you a ride back to D.C. or... ?"

"Are you nuts? I'll go back and get my stuff from his apartment on Monday after he's gone. I never want to see him again."

Music to my ears.

Upon opening my eyes the next morning, the first thing I saw was a blonde wig on the floor, and I suffered a spasm of dread, but then I turned my head cautiously and saw Jenny's dark tresses on the pillow, and it all came back to me. I held my breath as I stared at her, afraid to break the spell. What if she came to her senses this morning and remembered all the reasons she left before? I was still penniless and lacking any kind of career.

I could have continued in this negative line of thought, but Rufie must have sensed the master in need. Seeing me awake, and no doubt delighted by Jenny's familiar scent, he leapt onto the bed. She sat up laughing. Orson, not to be left out, sprang onto the foot of the bed and rubbed against her ankles. I didn't blame him a bit. It's just what I would have done if I were a cat.

Then she looked at me and smiled, and I smiled back, and it was, well, honestly, the mixture was almost too rich, if you know what I mean. Like flooding the engine of my heart. I kissed her to release some tension, but it didn't work. Then she looked into my eyes, and I saw that she was going say something serious, and the engine stalled.

"Duggie."

I waited, just staring at her, you know, kind of drinking it in, committing it to memory for future reference.

She was still smiling, at least. That had to be good, right?

"I never should have left."

Good start! "I've missed you so much," I said.

"I've missed you too. But..."

Damn.

"I still need to find a job. And there still aren't any jobs out here. So... I've been thinking maybe I'll room with Amanda for a while. She says there are a lot of jobs in Charlottesville."

I must have frowned, because she put her hand on my chest and starting talking, but of course I wasn't listening to every word then. Still, I think the gist was that she'd learned her lesson or something.

"So, I'd just stay there during the week and come out here every weekend."

"Okay," I said. Together every weekend was better than nothing. I'd take what I could get.

"So, what do you want to do today?" she asked.

I sat up fast. Work. Damn. I'd almost forgotten that I had to go in for brunch at the very least, but I told her I'd try to get out of the dinner shift. She said she'd be fine just hanging out at the shack with Rufie. She didn't mention Orson, but then, you don't have to spell things out for cats. They can read between the lines.

I was sitting at the counter in the café, nursing a second cup of coffee before heading into the kitchen, when a heavy hand slapped me between the shoulder blades.

"Whoa," I said, looking up at Witty, whose glistening black eye bulged from his face like an eight ball.

"Yeah, well, you should see the other guy."

"Which one? The last time I saw you it looked like you were fighting three or four."

He smirked. "Yeah. Those douche bags never had a chance. I'm just sorry I didn't get to crush that smart-ass bass player."

"Perhaps you shouldn't have tossed him off the stage so quickly."

"Hell. I thought he'd come back up to get even. The wimp disappeared."

"I think Cheyenne took charge of him."

Witty shook his head. "Women."

I eyed him carefully. His attempt at cynicism didn't fool me. If he was here on a Sunday morning, after having been left in the dust by the woman he'd been throwing himself at for the past month, it could only mean he'd already moved on.

"So, what brings you here?" I asked.

He shrugged and sat down on the stool next to me. The waitress brought him some coffee. He took a few gulps. Then he said, "After you left... after I saw Delilah makin' out with that slime ball, I realized that she wasn't the woman for me."

I nodded. "Yeah. She's kind of intense."

"Yeah." He seemed to be choosing his words carefully, which, for him, was something new. "You know how sometimes you can be looking right at something... or someone... and not even see it? Or them? I mean, you know what I mean."

I nodded again. "I think so."

He clunked the coffee cup down, sloshing a good portion of it on the counter. "The thing is, last night, after I'd finished teaching those wimps a lesson, I was walking to my truck, because, you know, I was feeling kind of low about... you know... women. And then this girl ran up to me. She ran, you know? Like she wasn't trying to play some game about being all hard-to-get and, you know, the way they do. You know her, this little girl, she was a cheerleader at the tournament—"

"You mean Phoebe?"

His face lit up. "Yeah. Phoebe. She's amazing."

I stared at him, marveling once again at the resilience of this sturdy veteran of the wrestling mat, whose heart had been rejected and kicked to the curb less than twenty-four hours ago, and here he was, a new lovelight shining in his one good eye.

"Yeah. She's a sweet girl," I said.

"You said that right. Sweet is what she is. She's everything that Delilah isn't. And get this, she told me last night that she didn't just fall in love with me when she saw me beating up those jerks. She said when she saw me cut up that tree—that big tree on the road?"

"Yeah, sure."

"She said she knew it then. But she'd heard that I was with Delilah. Then when she saw me walking away, and she saw that I was hurt..." He shook his head in wonder. "I'm telling you, Duggie, I don't know what I was thinking before, but this is the real thing. Phoebe loves me, man. She says I'm like Achilles."

"Really?" I forbore to fill him in on the whole story about the great warrior and his weakness, et cetera. Witty has many fine qualities, but an appreciation of the classics is not among them. "Well that's great. I'm happy for you both."

"That's good, man." He hesitated for a second, and then he said, "Phoebe told me how she used to have a thing for you. From back in high school. But, you should know, she's over it now." He looked me in the eye as if to let me know that any buried passion I might have been holding in reserve should be snuffed out now. I hastened to reassure him.

"I'm glad. I'm glad for both of you. Really. I think it's great you're together."

He nodded and punched my shoulder. "Thanks, man. I knew you'd understand."

During my shift that afternoon, I mused upon the way things had worked out. Although the band was more or less finished, at least in its former state, I felt that no blame could be assigned to me on that account. The seeds of discord were well rooted long before I came on the scene. And, who knows? Perhaps Goran and Nikolai would stay on with Jimmy and Denny and form some power cover band. Perhaps Matt would find happiness, or whatever it is he prefers in its stead, with some ultra-cool jazz group. I had no doubt that Delilah would let nothing stand in the way of her happiness. And as for Crater and Tucker, I didn't much care where life took them, as long as it took them someplace else.

Of course, now that I could no longer claim to be a band manager, I needed to come up with some new idea for making money that didn't involve washing dishes or teaching Latin, neither one of which provides a secure path to solvency. Still, with Jenny at my side, even if only on the weekends, how could I go wrong?

One thing still puzzled me, though. This business of Morris ferrying Jenny to the concert. How did that come about?

That evening, having begged for and gotten a reprieve from the dinner shift from Glory, who was feeling relatively chirpy since the cash flow was gurgling along nicely thanks to the successful leaf season, I suggested to Jenny that we stroll up to Morris's house. I didn't have to explain my motives to Jenny. She understands and tolerates my penchant for pot, even though she's not inclined that way herself.

Anyway, I had some questions for Morris, and once we'd covered the preliminary niceties of a social call, I waited until Jenny stepped into the kitchen to get a drink.

"So, Morris, I'm curious," I said, exhaling and passing him the joint. "How did you know that Jenny would come to the concert? You must have been pretty sure she would if you rented a costume before you even talked to her."

He didn't exactly smile, but he leaned back in his chair and lowered his eyelids in that kind of self-satisfied way he has. He took a long toke, held it, and let it out. Then he said, "When I was at the wine tasting, I noticed the way Brandon was looking at Delilah, and it occurred to me then that perhaps his feelings for Jenny weren't all they should be. I'd heard from friends that he was known as a bit of a skirt-chaser. I was also interested by Delilah's manner as she attempted to sing the great songs of the swing era. It seemed evident to me that, although she was able to read the lyrics, she had no insight into their great lyrical message of love and romance."

I frowned. Presumably there was a point in this, but so far, I wasn't getting it. In spite of his being an author of mystery novels, or perhaps because of it, Morris's discourse tends to suffer from a tendency to *obscurum per obscurius*—explanations which make things more obscure.

Perhaps noting this, Morris said, "I could see there was no romance in her soul. She struck me as the kind of girl who uses what she has to get what she wants. A woman like that is easily misled. I took the opportunity to chat with her after the event, telling her how much I admired her voice, and how she deserved a bigger audience. Then I asked if she'd ever considered how helpful a patron could be. I think at first she thought I was offering myself for the role, but eventually I put the suggestion to her that someone well connected in society, a popular artist such as Miles Brandon, for instance, could open doors for her."

I stared at him. I had no idea he could be so devious. I guess it must come from plotting those thrillers. No wonder he's such a success. You wouldn't have heard of him, because he writes under his nom de plume of Daphne Murdock, but Morris kicks ass on the bestseller lists.

"I wasn't sure if she'd taken the bait until you told me that Jenny wasn't going to be able to come to the concert, and the supposed reason why. I did some checking and discovered that Brandon had sent his regrets to the event he'd told her he had to attend. From that I deduced that he planned to see Delilah, and didn't want to be encumbered by Jenny. So I drove into town, rented a costume, and waited outside his apartment until I saw his car leave. You know the rest."

"Well I'll be," I said, staring at him. The magnitude of what he'd done, of how much I owed him—there was no way I could ever repay him.

"You'll be what?" said Jenny, walking back in from the kitchen holding a beer. She came over and sat next to me and put her hand on my thigh.

I stared at Morris. He was giving me that look. Like he knew what I was thinking. And I knew what he was thinking. And neither one of us had to say it out loud, but this time, I felt, his effort had been so far above and beyond the call of mere friendship, there was only one thing I could think of that might begin to show my gratitude.

It wasn't easy. But I knew it was the right thing to do.

"You know, Morris, I've been thinking," I said.

"It's never too late," he said.

I caught his eye. He was enjoying this. I sighed. I couldn't begrudge him. He'd earned it.

"You know I got that guitar because I was lonely without Jenny. But now... now that she's back, I guess I won't be needing it anymore, and I was wondering if you'd like to have it."

"Why Duggie, what a nice idea. I don't know what I'll do with it, but it's the thought that counts."

I had to smile. I know that he knows that I know that he knows, et cetera. But he was gracious in victory. He pulled out the good old pipe and passed it to me, saying. "This calls for a celebration, don't you think?"

See? He always knows what I'm thinking. Even when I'm not.

THE END

About the Author

Constance Harper Sprague was born in Erie, Pennsylvania, a quiet under-the-radar city with no illusions about itself. She continues to saunter to the beat of a different drummer in the Washington, D.C., area, where she remains a closet whistler, a lifelong daydreamer, and a competent roller skater. She is the author of a half dozen novels, most of them bearing little relation to reality.

Also By C.H. Sprague

POTLUCK
Second Edition
Silver Beech Press

"Not bad… Better than I could do!"
—P.R., Washington, DC

Love conquers almost all in this tale of bridled romance and lawless softball.

In the small town of Dudleigh, Virginia, what passes for social life reaches its apex each year at the Fourth of July softball tournament. Passions burn, tempers flare, and anything can happen in the tall grass.

Slacker extraordinaire and former Latin scholar Duggie Moon, captain of a team sponsored by his sister Glory's Moonlight Café, has his hands full after his ace pitcher and long-standing, unrequited love Jenny Carson is forced to play for the competition, and a team of ringers from out of town raises the stakes. To make matters worse, he's having trouble focusing because he's a little paranoid about the booming crop of pot he's secretly growing in an old school bus behind his house. All will be well if he can just get it harvested before anyone gets wind of it. But when the sheriff comes sniffing around the championship match and Duggie's got the game on his bat, all his plans could go up in smoke.